"So, how pregnant are you?"

"Pregnant!" Caitlin snapped.

Lucky rephrased the question. "How far along are you?"

"Three months."

That far. Three whole months Lucky had been an expectant father and didn't even know it. Hell, he didn't even know the mother.

"The baby's due in June."

The baby.

That soon.

"So what do we do about this?" he asked.

"I don't know."

That made two of them.

Dear Reader,

There is no bugle call more emotive or powerful than "Taps." It's played at the end of the day as a call to rest. In 1891 it became standard at military funerals. This honor is the final demonstration of a grateful nation to the families of those who served. The idea for *The Marine's Baby* came to me at a military funeral, but pieces of that story had been there all my life just waiting to be told.

My aunt hadn't been married long when her third husband died unexpectedly. My mother had been a young bride and pregnant with me when my father died. My aunt asked her how she'd managed to get through it all those years ago. My mother quoted my grandfather as saying, "This is the hardest thing you'll ever have to do, but you'll get through this, I promise." That became the premise for this book.

But even though I knew my heroine was going to be a young pregnant military widow-bride, I still needed my hero. As a veteran, I watch a lot of History Channel, Military Channel and war coverage. I also read every article I come across that has to do with today's military. I found it intriguing that men deploying under the threat of chemical and biological warfare were encouraged to put their semen in storage. I found it even more interesting that after the threat no longer existed babies were being fathered by men killed in action. The real heroes are the men and women who serve.

But I found the perfect hero for my heroine at a sperm bank. I hope you enjoy Caitlin and Lucky's story.

Rogenna Brewer

THE MARINE'S BABY
Rogenna Brewer

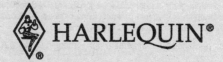

TORONTO • NEW YORK • LONDON
AMSTERDAM • PARIS • SYDNEY • HAMBURG
STOCKHOLM • ATHENS • TOKYO • MILAN • MADRID
PRAGUE • WARSAW • BUDAPEST • AUCKLAND

ISBN-13: 978-0-373-71478-0
ISBN-10:   0-373-71478-5

THE MARINE'S BABY

ABOUT THE AUTHOR

Best parenting advice ever received? Start and end each day with "I love you." **Favorite bedtime story?** *Goodnight Moon* by Margaret Wise Brown. As far as bedtime stories go, this one gets straight to the point. **Favorite lullaby?** "Return to Pooh Corner" by Kenny Loggins (as sung by Kenny, not me). **Keeper quote from your mom?** "Because I said so." **I wish my baby could've stayed forever at age...** I kind of like them all grown up. **Best reason behind a baby name...** My father died before I was born and my mother chose the name Roger (after him) for a boy and Genna (pronounced Gina) for a girl. I was named a hybrid Rogenna. **What makes a mom?** Eight arms and eyes in the back of the head help. **Most poignant moment...** The oldest two had gone off to school for the first day of kindergarten and first grade. I settled in to write the Great American Novel. My office was a 3x5 foot closet. I had to keep the door open because I'm claustrophobic. I had an apple-shaped plaque that said, "Mom's busy, take a number," complete with numbers for my sons. My youngest, who was a little bigger than a bundle at the time, stood outside my door until I noticed him. Needless to say, I didn't write a word that day. It took me years to finish that first book, but I never forgot that I was writing to stay home with them. Not because I was stuck at home with them.

Books by Rogenna Brewer

HARLEQUIN SUPERROMANCE

To Michael Arnold,
pharmacist extraordinaire… "Nice!"

And the cast of characters at WellDyne.
Miss you guys.

PROLOGUE

CryoBank of San Diego
Luke Calhoun Jr.
SSN#523XXXXXX
August 29, 2007

Dear Service Member:

When our military readied you to deploy, CBSD stepped forward to ensure the future of your family by providing semen collection and storage services free of charge for the first year. We would like to continue to serve you as you continue to serve our country.

Thank you for choosing CryoBank of San Diego. We understand the importance of your decision. Please take a moment to consider your future family dreams.

__Continue to store my specimen for the discounted military rate of $350.00 for one year.

__Donate my specimen.

__Destroy my specimen.

Sincerely,
Carol Livingston, Director CBSD
Visa and MasterCard accepted

CAITLIN STOOD AT THE MAILBOX outside the home she was in the process of vacating and reread the letter addressed to her late husband, Lieutenant Luke Calhoun, United States Navy. She'd barely been a bride before she'd become a widow.

Luke had been a Navy SEAL killed in action.

Eighty-nine days, nine hours and nine minutes ago two men in uniform had come knocking on her door. One of these days she'd stop counting down to the minute, but right now she had less than sixty of them before the military housing inspector arrived to sign off on her departure from officers' row.

The single-story house looked like every other house on the block, but it was the only home she and Luke had ever known together. The military had given her written notice and ninety days to vacate the premises. That deadline was today and Caitlin was up to her Playtex gloves in cleaning, which needed to be done in short order.

Movers were coming and going around her. She didn't have time to stop and think about how much she missed eyes so green and so full of life her heart ached whenever she looked at the emerald-and-diamond engagement ring nestled against her wedding band.

Still, she needed a moment to collect her thoughts. Freeing her long blond hair from the loose black band, she reread the letter again. Her heart pounded with the implication.

Sperm bank. CryoBank was a sperm bank.

And her husband had made a deposit without telling her? Her husband had done a lot of things he didn't talk to her about—that was the nature of his business—but this?

He should have told her about his semen in storage. They'd never discussed children, except to acknowledge that they both wanted them—someday. Well, *someday* had arrived for Caitlin.

She didn't know whether to skip up the street and kiss the mail carrier on his bald head, or sink down to the curb for a good cry. Or maybe both.

"Pete!" she called out, realizing she'd forgotten to give him her change-of-address form. By this time tomorrow she'd be boarding a plane for Maryland. Home to her father. She didn't belong in California anymore, as evidenced by the number of Navy wives who hadn't shown up to help her pack. Women she'd once called friends had separated themselves from the grim reminder of her reality. The Casualty Assistance duo could come knocking on any one of their doors next.

She belonged to a new sorority now. They dressed in black, listened to sad songs and watched far more war coverage than they should. Or couldn't watch it at all without crying.

War widows.

She met Pete—dispatcher of correspondence and sound advice—in the middle of the street, surprising him with a peck on the cheek. "Thank you, thank you so much for everything."

"And just what am I supposed to tell the missus about the lipstick on my collar?" he teased as Caitlin went skipping back across the street.

"Tell her you just delivered the best news of my *life!*" Twenty-four was way too young to be spending that life alone. Caitlin hurried back to the house, weaving her way between movers. Two coming. Two going.

"Not that box." Pam, Caitlin's one true friend, redirected the barrel-chested driver. He turned around and set it down inside the door before going farther into the house for another.

Pam followed him around the corner to the back bedroom while Caitlin, still holding on to hope with that bundle of mail, stopped to lift a cardboard flap. She knew she shouldn't. This was the box filled with Luke's uniforms and destined for the thrift store on base.

She had the flag that draped his casket. His medals. His letters of commendation. Her memories.

Those were the things she'd allowed herself to keep.

But after all the hours spent sorting through the things she couldn't, it was his uniforms that were the hardest to part with. She knew she shouldn't, but she dug out one of his desert-drab T-shirts that had been sent home from Iraq and buried her nose in it. How dare he still linger to torture her this way? She needed him now more than ever, and all she had to hold on to was this damn ugly khaki T-shirt.

"Caitlin?" Pam tucked a strand of dark hair behind her ear. The bobbed cut was as practical as the woman herself.

"Just this one." Caitlin held tightly to Luke's T-shirt.

She'd met him the first day of spring at the Annapolis Yacht Club's traditional burning of the socks—after which no member could be caught wearing socks with their deck shoes.

He'd been a guest lecturer at the Naval Academy.

She'd been a bored debutante/grad student who thought he looked good in his uniform. It had been love at first sight.

After a brief courtship they'd married in a lavish spring wedding, followed by a honeymoon in the Caribbean. Then came her move to San Diego. His deployment to the Middle East.

By summer she was a widow.

"I'm not ready to let him go."

"Oh, honey," Pam sympathized. "I know. But you have to…"

Not if she had his baby.

Luke's baby.

Was she really considering having his baby alone?

"…oh, look at the time," Pam said, checking her watch. "I have to pick up the boys from school."

"Of course," Caitlin said as her friend deserted her for the responsibilities of single parenthood—*single,* meaning Pam's husband was deployed. She was not by any stretch of the imagination really alone and would never understand the direction of Caitlin's thoughts. So Caitlin kept those thoughts to herself.

"This is the hardest thing you'll ever have to do," her father had said as he'd walked her down the aisle for a second time, this time toward her husband's coffin.

"But you'll get through this, I promise. No major decisions, Caitie. Not for the next year at least. Give yourself time to grieve."

Caitlin ignored her father's good advice and let all the past-due bills and collection notices fall to the floor. But she held on to that T-shirt and that letter from CryoBank. Luke had promised her the world. Apparently he'd gone into debt trying to give it to her. Did he think he had to buy her love? He'd been such a gentle and generous lover, how could she not have loved him?

But she had a funny feeling she never really knew him.

"Please take a moment to consider…"

Future. Family. Dreams. She was going to have his baby. Before she forgot what it was like to dream about the future, to have a future.

Caitlin winced at the three-week-old postmark. Like most of Luke's mail, the letter had been forwarded from his Command. She only hoped she wasn't too late.

"One last gift, Luke." Her words echoed off the ceiling and the empty walls as she punched the numbers from the letterhead into her cell phone.

She didn't even hear the mover coming up behind her until he cleared his throat. "Will that be all, Mrs. Calhoun?"

CryoBank of San Diego
Luke Calhoun Jr.
SSN#523XXXXXX
August 29, 2007

Dear Service Member:

When our military readied you to deploy, CBSD stepped forward to ensure the future of your family by providing semen collection and storage services free of charge for the first year. We would like to continue to serve you as you continue to serve our country.

Thank you for choosing CryoBank of San Diego. We understand the importance of your decision. Please take a moment to consider your future family dreams.

__Continue to store my specimen for the discounted military rate of $350.00 for one year.

__Donate my specimen.

__Destroy my specimen.

Sincerely,
Carol Livingston, Director CBSD
Visa and MasterCard accepted

HEADED BACK TO HIS TENT AFTER mail call, Master Sergeant "Lucky" Luke Calhoun Jr., United States Marine Corps, put his X next to *destroy* with the nubby pencil he carried on patrol. He was too cheap to cough up three-fifty and, after four tours in the Middle East, too jaded to think he could make anyone's dreams come true.

He'd be happy if everyone just stopped killing each other—a strange sentiment for a guy who spent most of his time at the beautiful Desert Palms Resort, aka Camp Victory, Baghdad, Iraq, looking through the cross-hairs of a sniper's scope. He did his job, and he did it well. That didn't mean he had to like it.

Besides, he was ready for a change of scenery.

Pushing back the tent flap, Lucky ducked inside.

Private "Tick" Tanner lay stretched out on his rack, reading a letter with the identifiable CryoBank logo. He looked up as Lucky walked in. "You get one, Sarg?"

"Everyone in the unit got one." Tossing his mail aside, Lucky sat down on his own rack and stowed his rifle in the folds of the wool blanket beneath. The blanket kept the sand out of his weapon. Or at least it was supposed to.

Nothing could keep the sand out in the desert.

They ate it. Drank it. Slept in it. Even breathed it in. War was one hell of a dirty job, no matter how you looked at it.

"So you gonna, you know, pay for storage?"

Without the imminent threat of biological warfare, it seemed like a waste of money. "No."

"Tick, Tick." Sergeant Eddie Estes sauntered over with a care package from home. "You don't know Lucky. He's so cheap, when they handed out the specimen cups he—"

Lucky cut him off with a glare.

Estes mouthed, "*twice*," and held up two fingers.

"Very funny," Lucky said without humor.

Grinning, Estes tossed a can of Pringles his way. Lucky caught it in midair. From the sound of it he was going to be munching more crumbs than chips.

"Were we supposed to fill those cups?" Tick looked from one to the other.

"Dumbshit." Estes threw another can and beaned the kid in the head. Maybe Tick had been hit in the head once too often. Or maybe he was just that young. Lucky's money was on *that young*.

The kid was barely nineteen.

"So, Eddie," Tick said, "you're not going to pay for storage, either?"

"They want a piece of me—" Estes plopped down on his own rack and opened a can of sour cream and onion "—they can pay me just like they would any other slob off the street."

"CryoBank isn't in the free-storage business," Lucky felt compelled to point out.

"But what if..." Tick started to say. "You know—"

Lucky was ready to put an end to this conversation. He never let himself think about the *what if*. Some guys believed every tour after the third was borrowed time. Lucky wasn't the superstitious type. But he believed in making his own luck. "You don't have to make up your mind right this minute," he reassured Tick. "Why don't you sleep on it?"

Lucky didn't have that luxury. Half his mail was from a collection agency and didn't even belong to him. And he did have to deal with his *little* problem sooner rather than later.

He opened the first collection notice. Normally, he wouldn't open someone else's mail. But when that someone was his dead half brother—his dead half brother with his same name—well, he felt entitled. The mail mix-up was happening more often now that *Little Luke* had been KIA.

In the past they'd forwarded any misdirected mail directly to the other with a brotherly, *thank-you-very-much* note attached. Except *thanks* wasn't the real sentiment. At least not on his part. Lucky felt the shame of his resentment burning a hole in his gut. He was the older brother. He should have been the bigger man.

The George Foreman brothers had nothing on the Luke Calhoun boys. The Foremans had a father who had given them his name because he loved them. Lucky's own father didn't know the meaning of love.

At least not with his pants zipped.

Growing up, Lucky had been Junior. Luke had come along four years later as Little Luke because Big Luke's secretary had wanted everyone to know the father of her baby. As if there had been any doubt. That had ended Lucky's parents' marriage around the same time Lucky's baby brother, Bruce, was born.

Big Luke's secretary became the second Mrs. Luke Calhoun Senior. Little Luke became the favorite son while Junior became the forgotten one.

After that Lucky stopped going by Junior.

Eventually, Big Luke's brother, John, had moved in— which was how Lucky's uncle became his stepfather. Years later another half brother—or was that first cousin? He was never quite sure which—was born. By the time Lucky's mother had Keith the town gossips couldn't wag their tongues fast enough.

Calhouns were bad blood.

Lucky shuffled the first collection notice to the back and opened the next one. But he couldn't stop thinking about Luke. The home wrecker had finally packed up Little Luke and moved away, while Big Luke had moved on to Mrs. Luke Calhoun Senior number three. There were no more half sibs—that Lucky knew of, anyway—but with his father being fifty-five, with a wife two decades younger, it still wasn't out of the question.

As soon as Lucky had turned seventeen, he'd left Englewood, Colorado, without looking back. That had been fifteen years ago.

He kept in touch with Bruce and Keith. Called his mother twice a year, on her birthday and Mother's Day. Never spoke to his uncle, because neither of them were talkers. Or his father. Heard all the family gossip through their sister, his crazy aunt Dottie. And until Luke had been killed, Lucky had never felt a twinge of anything familial for his two half brothers.

Maybe he was incapable of love.

At least with his pants zipped.

Glancing at the bills in his hand, Lucky took a deep breath and let it out again. Three months ago the chaplain had woken him from a sound sleep to inform him of his family's double tragedy.

Like Lucky, Bruce was a Marine. But like Luke, Bruce had gone through SEAL training and the two were with the same Navy SEAL team when it happened.

Luke had lost his life.

Bruce had lost his leg.

With two Calhouns down for the count and one too young to enlist, Lucky had earned a free ride home—if he wanted it, which he did. And home to him meant his adopted home in California, not his home of record in Colorado.

But he didn't take it.

He didn't want to earn his ticket that way. Instead, he chose to stay at the Desert Palms Resort, where the bulk of his mail came in the form of past-due bills and collection notices belonging to a dead man. A man he'd never called brother.

Today's bills were the third and final notices from a jewelry store. The twelve-thousand-dollar diamond-and-emerald engagement ring had an unpaid balance of over six thousand dollars with interest and late fees.

Mail in hand, Lucky picked up his Pringles canister and headed for the long Internet access lines. He had two Morale, Welfare and Recreation buildings to choose from—Area 51 and Dodge City. He headed in the direction of building 51F. Free Internet access, commercial phones and televisions were just a few of the perks of modern warfare. He preferred the hardships of an FOB, Forward Operating Base, as a reminder of why he was here.

But today he didn't mind the conveniences.

While in line, explosions rumbling in the background, he read his only other piece of mail.

Dear Lucky,

I hear Keith made his high school basketball team. I remember how much you boys loved that game. Do you get the chance to "shoot hoops" in Iraq? Of course, Bruce was a much better player than you were. You were always so damn big and clumsy, bumping into the other boys, and fouling out so often you spent entire games warming the bench.

"It's called defense, Dottie." Bruce had been an offensive forward, leading scorer—and four years too young for them to ever have competed on the same court. Same with Luke.

That is, until the three of them wound up in Iraq. He'd have to remember to tell his aunt about their night games under the floodlights. Of course, Bruce was back in California now.

Anyway, good for Keith. Lucky continued reading....

I suppose Bruce won't be playing much basketball after losing his leg, not to mention losing his fiancée. I heard she took one look at the stump and went running from the hospital room. Well, good riddance is all I can say. Speaking of which, the Navy kicked the widow-bride out of housing. Gave her ninety days to vacate. I would have gone out there to help pack, but my bursitis has been acting up again.

Flew out with Nora Jean for the funeral. Your father showed up, and naturally they had words. Can't be civil to each other for more than two minutes, not even for the dearly departed. Good thing your uncle John was there to keep the peace. Keith, too. I can understand why your mother wasn't, with Bruce being in the hospital and all, but I can't understand why the Marine Corps wouldn't give you leave to bury your own brother.

Nora Jean is beside herself with grief. Hasn't gotten

*out of bed since the funeral, and it was such a touching
ceremony with all the military formalities. Though I
think the widow-bride should hand over the flag to her
mother-in-law. It would be a lovely gesture. After all,
Little Luke and his bride knew each other only three
short months and Nora Jean's been mother to that boy
all his life.*

*There's only one reason for a young couple to rush
to the altar like that, but if she's pregnant she isn't
showing. A shame if she isn't—and I don't think she is—
because what a comfort that would be. Now that I think
about it, ninety days is just about right for the Navy to
send the widow-bride packing.*

*Maybe I'll drop her a note and suggest she do just
that, about the flag, I mean. Then I'll send her over to
the naval hospital to visit Bruce. You know how much
those two boys looked alike. And here they went from
being on rival high school basketball teams to being on
the same Navy SEAL team. Now wouldn't it be something if Bruce and the widow-bride found some comfort
in each other?*

*Love,
Aunt Dottie*

It'd be something, all right. And not something good.
Just something else to keep the tongues wagging.

By the time Lucky finished his aunt's letter he'd moved to
the head of the line and sat down at the bank of computers
with the widow-bride on his mind.

Her real name was Catherine or Caitlin, something like

that. But in Calhoun family lore she'd forever be known as Little Luke's widow-bride. He didn't know much about her, other than she came from old money back east.

Maryland, maybe? That's where Luke had met her, anyway.

His advice to the widow would be to surrender the flag. It'd be worth it to get Nora Jean out of her life.

Getting rid of Aunt Dottie, on the other hand, would be impossible. For a man who'd grown up without any real sense of family, that thought was as comforting as it was discomforting.

Once online, instead of the form letter the JAG office had prepared and a copy of the death certificate the chaplain had provided, he accessed his bank account and paid the damn jewelry-store bill. No woman should be stuck with the bill for her own engagement ring. Between Nora Jean and Dottie, the widow-bride would have enough on her plate.

That didn't stop him from wincing as he hit the transaction button that would deplete his savings account by some six thousand dollars. Money was one thing a tightwad didn't part with easily. Especially when he was saving up for something special.

Tick really didn't know him if he didn't know that much about him, at least. Three hundred and fifty dollars for sperm storage? No, thanks.

He had ninety days left before he was out of here, and out of the service for good. He'd made it this far; he could keep his balls tucked tight for another three months.

He was lucky that way.

After that, he'd chuck his fifteen-year military career, buy that Harley he'd always wanted and spend a year doing nothing except taking his freedom for granted.

CHAPTER ONE

CAITLIN SANK TO THE COOL TILE floor of her tiny apartment bathroom, waiting for the nausea to subside. The crackers she kept on her nightstand helped some, but then she had to put up with crumbs in her bed.

Crumbs were a poor substitute for a warm body.

Her decision to stay in California had been rash, but not one she regretted, even though turning the moving van around had created a logistical nightmare. She'd had to find a place fast. Store everything from the three-bedroom row house that didn't fit into her new one-bedroom apartment. And redirect Luke's and her mail to the new address. Not to mention how disappointed her father had been when she'd cashed in her ticket and told him she wouldn't be coming home. She might not belong in this state anymore, but Coronado was where she'd buried her heart. And California was where she'd chosen to stay.

She had a meeting "of a serious nature" with CryoBank director Carol Livingston at eleven, followed by lunch with "the wives" at noon. And here she could barely pull herself together long enough to get dressed.

She stretched Luke's T-shirt across her legs, resting her forehead against her raised knees. The Navy had come knocking 184 days and seven hours ago.

His scent had faded. So had her memories. Now whenever she wanted to picture his face she had to look at an actual picture of him.

"I'm not ready." Not ready to let him go? Or not ready to go it alone?

Pregnancy was *not* the joyous event she'd imagined it to be. Not when Luke wasn't here to share it with her. She felt more alone than she ever would have thought possible. And more afraid. She had yet to tell her friends.

They weren't even her friends anymore, not really. But she had to tell somebody before she burst at the seams, literally. She needed them to feel happy for her, since she couldn't quite allow herself those feelings yet.

And what if they weren't happy for her?

What if, like her father, they thought she'd rushed into things? He wanted her home. But she wanted to at least try to make it on her own first. Before the wedding, he'd been critical of her marrying so young and of her moving so far away—but he'd come around after meeting Luke.

And he'd come around about the baby. But her mother-in-law? Caitlin was a mess just thinking about it.

No, her mother-in-law was a mess.

Since the death of her only child, Nora Jean loved Caitlin one minute and hated her the next. Scratch that. The woman had always hated her and no longer bothered to keep up the pretense. No woman, except maybe one she'd handpicked, would ever have been good enough for her Little Luke. The woman had had much higher political aspirations for her son's naval career. Which was why she'd told everyone Caitlin was from "old money" when she wasn't.

Nora Jean had gone ballistic when she'd learned Caitlin was the beneficiary of his stored semen. No telling how she'd react to the news that Caitlin had actually put those sperm to good use. The woman had tried to exert control over Caitlin's every decision since Luke's death.

And then there was Dottie. Luke's aunt actually had the nerve to suggest that Caitlin give his flag to his mother.

His flag!

Nora Jean had had her pick of Luke's personal possessions, but Caitlin drew the line at his flag and his future babies. His mother had a deep-seated fear that given time, Caitlin would remarry and these things would become meaningless to her. Her mother-in-law didn't know her very well. She would always love Luke.

She pushed herself up from the bathroom floor with the uneasy feeling that no one was going to react quite the way she wanted them to.

She could just imagine what CryoBank wanted.

While her husband's initial deposit had been free, she'd found withdrawal and continued storage of his remaining specimen to be quite expensive but necessary if she wanted to give her child a little brother or sister someday.

She'd opted for the credit card payment plan, which was probably in default by now. Someone had canceled all her credit cards, but the bills just kept coming.

Removing her rings, Caitlin set them in the soap dish next to the sink. The only time she could remember being that frivolous with money was when it came to her wedding. Even then her father had footed the bill, just as he had for all seven years of her college education—at least those things not covered by the scholarships she'd earned. And while she wouldn't call the University of Maryland a frivolous expense, it sure felt like it when she wasn't putting that education to work for her.

Caitlin turned on the shower. The responsibilities of single parenthood would be her reality soon enough. Stripping while waiting for the tepid water to heat, she hesitated over the hamper with Luke's T-shirt in hand and buried her face in it one last time.

She'd been a widow for almost six months. Pregnant for three. Longer than they'd been married. Longer than she'd even known him.

Maybe if she didn't wear his T-shirt any more she could preserve what was left of him.

Catching a glimpse of herself in the mirror, Caitlin put a hand to the slight swell of her belly. She had loved and cherished her husband in life.

A baby was how she would honor him in death.

She didn't need to wear a ratty old rag anymore, and tossed it into the hamper to prove it.

AN HOUR LATER CAITLIN WAS ushered into Carol Livingston's poinsettia-filled office. In a state where street-corner Santas dressed more like surfers, Caitlin had almost forgotten this was the week before Christmas.

"Come in, Mrs. Calhoun. Caitlin." The CryoBank director opened yet another door, leading from her paneled office to a windowless boardroom. Two men stood as the women entered.

Their names escaped Caitlin as soon as they introduced themselves as attorneys with the law firm of such and such.

"Carol?" she asked with the same mock familiarity the woman had used with her. "What's going on?"

Surely these men had better things to do than harass her for past-due storage and withdrawal fees.

"Perhaps you'd better sit down," the woman suggested.

Uh-oh. That didn't sound good. Caitlin's knees buckled at the precise moment one of the lawyers rolled a padded leather chair underneath her. Thankfully, it broke her fall.

But he may as well have pulled it out from under her when he said, "It's my duty to inform you, Mrs. Calhoun, that you were impregnated with the semen of a man other than your late husband."

Caitlin looked from him to the other two. "What? Would you mind repeating…" He couldn't possibly have said what she thought he'd just said. It just wasn't possible. A minute ago she'd walked through the door, pregnant with Luke's baby. Now he was telling her…

"The baby you're carrying is not your husband's."

The blood drained from her face, leaving her light-headed. *Not Luke's baby?*

Caitlin doubled over, and someone shoved her head between her knees. They were talking to her and at her and around her, but she couldn't understand a word they were saying.

She started to hyperventilate and Carol Livingston called her secretary to bring a paper bag. The younger woman rushed in and pushed a crinkled sack into Caitlin's face. "Breathe!"

From between her knees, Caitlin held the bag to her nose and mouth. It smelled like a tuna-fish sandwich. Normally she liked tuna, but under the circumstances it turned her stomach.

"Breathe, Caitlin," the director ordered. "That a girl. Breathe into the bag."

In and out. In and out.

Eventually she sat back up.

In. The brown bag emptied. "Sperm banks do not make those kinds of mistakes," she muttered through the paper. Out. The brown bag inflated. "I read your brochure cover to cover." Removing the smelly sack, she looked from one to the other. "You use a handprint reader—"

The biometric identification device recorded a 3-D measurement of the donor's hand. Along with the computerized system, the sensor identified a donor by his handprint and not just by a number or a card.

"This was a clerical error unique to our military deployment project and the processing of thousands of men at one time...." Carol cleared her throat. "Your doctor's office received the wrong sample. I assure you nothing like this has ever happened before—"

"But you're saying it *has* happened. *To me!*"

"We will, of course, cover any and all expenses related to this pregnancy," the lawyer who'd pulled out her chair said.

"And/or termination." This from the one who had been quiet until now. He circled to the opposite side of the table, where he sat down across from her. "If you so choose," he added as if that were a foregone conclusion.

Caitlin put a protective hand on her stomach.

She wore a fitted black, button-down shirt with three-quarter sleeves untucked over black slacks. An outfit she'd chosen because the feminine flare gave her room to breathe.

But at the moment it felt uncomfortably tight around the un-buttoned waistband.

She didn't like the quiet lawyer so much.

He pushed a piece of paper across the mahogany table toward her. "This check should be more than enough to cover your expenses. You just need to sign here…."

It was a generous offer but not *that* generous. She'd be a fool to accept it. She needed to talk to someone.

"Who *is* the father?"

"I'm afraid we have to protect our donor's anonymity," Carol Livingston said. "But he has been contacted and should he wish to get in touch with you we can make that arrangement—"

"What about my anonymity?"

"It's up to you—"

"If it were up to me—" Caitlin cut herself off.

She didn't know what she'd been about to threaten.

She didn't sound very threatening.

She sounded…terrified.

Closing her eyes, she took a couple more deep breaths. "I don't know," she muttered in a somewhat calmer tone. Much calmer than she was feeling. "I don't know anything about him."

"I can have one of our techs pull up some data. I'm afraid our military profiles are not as comprehensive as our donor profiles, which include baby pictures, family medical histories and several personality tests. You'll find out little more than the color of his hair and his eyes."

"I'm afraid I'm going to have to insist you sign this paper first, Mrs. Calhoun," the not-so-quiet lawyer said.

Was she really going to sell out for the color of the father's eyes? Caitlin brushed her engagement ring with her thumb. Working the center stone around, she closed her fist over those diamonds and emeralds until she felt them dig into her palm.

"Caitlin," Carol Livingston said, breaking through her thoughts, "while I can't legally or ethically give you a name, before you make any decisions about the pregnancy I do want you to know that this man and your husband share genetic markers that suggest they're related. Very closely related."

"How close?" Caitlin demanded.

The loud lawyer with the check cleared his throat.

The director hesitated, looking to him for direction.

"Possibly a first cousin. Or a half brother," the lawyer who had pulled out her chair spoke up.

"My husband doesn't have any brothers. Or cousins…" Actually, that wasn't true. The funeral was just a blur, but Luke's father had been there with family…. His third wife, Maddie. His sister, Dottie. A brother, John.

And John had a teenaged son, Keith.

Keith would be a first cousin.

But not a sperm donor.

Caitlin would have invited her groom's family to the wedding, but Luke had produced a list with only two names. His mother and his aunt. Naturally she'd assumed there were no other living relatives. Even then he'd spent the entire reception keeping her away from the woman he'd called his crazy aunt.

Caitlin didn't even know his father was alive until after the honeymoon when Luke said something that made her realize they were estranged, otherwise etiquette would have demanded they invite him. But her dream of reconciling father and son was lost along with her husband.

Luke Senior, or rather Big Luke, as he'd insisted on being called at the funeral, had one of those booming personalities that couldn't be ignored. Nora Jean had had the bad manners to pick a fight with her ex-husband at their son's funeral. But Caitlin's own father had been there to protect her from the worst of it. And someone, she thought maybe Big Luke's brother, John, had escorted Luke's father out the door.

Big Luke was on his third wife. Did that mean he had three families? And how many sons?

The pushy lawyer clicked his ballpoint pen.

All Caitlin wanted was out of this room. Her heart was pounding. Her head was pounding.

There was no question in her mind she was going to keep this baby. This baby that wasn't Luke's. No, this baby that was Luke's no matter what they said.

Oh, Luke.

Brother. Cousin. Hope.

She touched the check, looked at the amount again. Thirty-five thousand dollars. She could get through the pregnancy with that money. Or she could walk out of here with nothing. Contact an attorney of her own. Sue for even more money. Wait months or even years before she saw a dime. While her private life became a public spectacle?

She took the offered pen, but still she hesitated.

What was she doing?

"And, of course," the pushy lawyer continued, "if you sign the check, all future storage fees will be waived. If not, all past-due receipts will have to be paid today or your husband's specimen will be destroyed."

Was he *blackmailing* her? With her dead husband's semen? She did not like this guy one bit. Caitlin scribbled her name on the dotted line and sensed the relief from the others. All Caitlin felt was a wave of nausea that all the crackers in the world wouldn't settle.

Without another word Caitlin picked up the check, and Carol Livingston handed her off to her secretary. With a quiet click, the director's office door closed behind her. The secretary in turn walked Caitlin down the hall and handed her off to one of a half-dozen very busy techs.

The young woman turned over a document with all personal data blacked out. The simple form had been filled out by hand.

He was thirty-two years old.

Caucasian male.

Brown hair. Green eyes.

Height: 6'3". Weight: 229 lbs.

Except for the age difference—Luke had been twenty-eight—the description fit her husband perfectly.

The DNA comparisons provided even less info. She had no idea what she was looking at. Pictures of actual chromosomes? Forty-six chromosomes, twenty-three pairs. What did that tell her? Biology had been one of her two favorite subjects throughout school. Still, as a bio-chem major, she was no expert in genetics.

"I'm afraid I don't know what any of this means." There was a chart of some kind with two lines running superimposed over similar peaks and valleys. In the top right-hand corner, the chart listed twenty as the overall percentage of matching genetic markers. "Where does it say half brother or first cousin?"

"Mathematically," the tech explained, "if two men are half siblings, twenty-five percent of their genes should be identical, first cousins, twelve and a half percent. But because inheritance is random, any given gene could be compared to a coin toss."

"In other words this could be a cousin *or* a half brother?"

The tech set the chromosome shots side by side. "The Y chromosome is the only genetic information that is identical in males of the same father. All male relatives of paternal lineage share the same Y chromosome."

This man and her husband had the same Y chromosome.

Caitlin looked at the profile again. So eerily similar to Luke's.

"Can I see my husband's profile?"

"Sure," the young woman said without hesitation, then disappeared into a room behind the desk. Beyond an open door, a tech was guiding a couple through the online donor selection process.

Behind Caitlin, a young man walked in, put his palm to the sensor in the corner and punched in some numbers. At first glance, the device resembled an ATM machine. He grabbed his label printout and headed toward the back, stopping to joke with one of the techs. A red light changed to green as a man exited one of the rooms and handed off his labeled specimen through a tiny door. A cleaning woman moved in and out of the open rooms.

Busy place.

And everywhere she looked she saw poinsettia-themed holiday decorations. Suddenly, she felt very homesick. Flying home for Christmas didn't seem like such a bad idea. Caitlin blinked back tears. This would have been her first Christmas as Luke's wife. Instead, it was her first Christmas as his widow. She wasn't a crier. But with her hormones out of whack, there was no telling when the floodgates would open.

A harried man in a business suit rushed in with a brown paper bag. He paused at the handprint sensor to get his printout, then proceeded to instruct a tech that his specimen was to be delivered to his wife's doctor the following week when he would be out of town on business. Over the holidays? Maybe if he wasn't such a workaholic…

Then again, who was she to criticize?

If her husband hadn't been a Navy SEAL…

If, if, if!

Caitlin's tech reappeared with a thick three-ring binder labeled *CA L*. She knew a little something about medical coding.

CA L for Calhoun, Luke?

The young woman flipped through a few pages then set the open book on the counter in front of Caitlin.

Luke Calhoun Jr.

"This isn't—" Caitlin looked up and realized the tech was no longer standing in front of her. The young woman was busy answering the telephone and appeared to be the only one covering the front desk at the moment. This wasn't her husband's profile. But it looked vaguely familiar.

Her husband wasn't a Junior. Why *not?*

Technically, it meant he and his father didn't share a middle name. So, then, why was his father Luke Senior? Because he had another son? A son who shared his full name?

Caitlin flipped forward a page and found her Luke.

His profile. His handwriting.

She traced the bold strokes with her finger and a longing that made her heart ache. Her husband's middle name was Lane, his mother's maiden name, but it wasn't listed.

She flipped forward a few more pages. The book was chock-full of Calhouns, including several Luke Calhouns. A common enough name. Was that the root of the clerical error? Or something more complicated? Her heartbeat sped up as she flipped back to Luke Calhoun Jr. No middle name listed there, either.

His page looked familiar because it was identical to the profile she'd been handed earlier. Only the personal information wasn't blacked out on this original.

This was the guy.

Caitlin looked up. The young tech looked right at her, then glanced away. She knew. She knew something. And she'd given Caitlin this opportunity, maybe her only opportunity, to steal this piece of personal information.

Oh God, she was going to go to jail for the misuse of medical records. Okay, so maybe that was an exaggeration, but she was certainly putting her professional career on the line. Was it worth it? *Well, duh!*

Same handwriting. Same everything.

Except now she knew his name, rank and serial number.

A serviceman's serial number was his social security number. The first three digits identified the state. Every military wife knew her husband's social security number by heart, and 523 was the same state in which her husband had been born— Colorado. There wasn't a chance she'd forget his name or his state of birth. She quickly memorized the six digits that followed.

Another tech stepped back into the room.

"I'm taking these." Caitlin picked up the useless copies she'd been given, ready to spring for the door with the information she'd obtained with the help of… She read the tech's name tag. "Thank you, Jenny."

"Merry Christmas, Mrs. Calhoun." Jenny walked over and closed the book. "Navy wives should stick together, don't you think?"

CAITLIN DROVE TO THE Officer's Club on autopilot. She was running too late to cancel lunch. Though she wanted to talk to someone, anyone, under the circumstances she couldn't break the news of her pregnancy to a group of Navy wives. She didn't even know how she was going to make it through an hour of polite conversation.

As expected, the three women were waiting out front. Pam stood under a decorated palm tree, checking her cell phone messages.

They didn't notice Caitlin pull up in her yellow '64 1/2 Mustang convertible. Her father had gone to a great deal of expense to restore the car down to its red, pony interior. At least with the check in her bag she'd no longer have to sell her graduation present. Luke's Ford F-150 had already been repossessed.

God, how he'd loved that truck.

The wives didn't notice her when she got out of the car. When she stepped onto the curb. And not when she came to an abrupt halt on the sidewalk only a few feet away. They were too busy dissing her.

"She's put on weight." Marilyn, who was rail thin and always on a diet, would notice that. "I think she's pregnant."

Jill rolled her eyes. "She can't be. Do the math."

"Then what was she doing at the ob/gyn a couple months ago?" Marilyn looked smug.

"There could be any number of reasons why she'd see a doctor," Jill argued. "Her annual physical for one."

"A fertility specialist?" Marilyn *tsked*.

"Seriously?" Pam looked up from her messages. "She did receive one of those letters from CryoBank. I recognized the letterhead from the flyers plastered all over base."

Jill's mouth gaped open. "You don't think…"

Marilyn lifted an eyebrow. "Oh, I think…"

Caitlin listened as her friends drew their own conclusions. Then her cell phone rang.

Pam looked up, then at the phone in her hand, unable to comprehend that her thumb had pressed the button that had given Caitlin away. They all stared at Caitlin.

"I guess you already know my news." She turned on her heel and headed back to her car.

"Caitlin," Pam called after her. "Wait! What were you thinking?"

SHE DIDN'T KNOW WHAT SHE WAS thinking. Back home in her sparsely furnished apartment without a holiday decoration in sight, Caitlin turned off the ringer on her cell phone and ignored her ringing home phone.

It was either another bill collector or Pam. Again.

She didn't want to deal with either of them right now. She needed all her courage to make the next phone call.

Every military wife knew to keep the number for the American Red Cross by the telephone in case of emergencies.

Caitlin punched in that number right away, before her phone started ringing again. If this wasn't an emergency, she didn't know what was.

"American Red Cross," the volunteer answered.

"I'd like to send a health and welfare message to a service member."

"And what is his or her name, please?"

"Luke Calhoun *Junior*." Caitlin said the name out loud for the first time, making it all too real. This *really* wasn't happening. Any moment now she'd wake up next to Luke and he'd tell her it was all a bad dream, then life would go on as it should—happily ever after.

"Service number?"

Caitlin rattled off the numbers she'd memorized.

"Your name and relationship?"

"Caitlin Calhoun. *Mrs.* Caitlin Calhoun," she emphasized, skipping over the relationship part, letting the woman make the natural assumption.

"And your message, Mrs. Calhoun?"

"I just found out I'm pregnant. I'd like to tell him that. And…and get him to call me," she added.

"Congratulations." She could sense the woman smiling over the phone as her fingers flew over the keyboard. "And your husband's command?"

"I—I don't know. I mean, we're new to the base." Well, sort of. She *had* been new to the base. Now she wasn't even on the base.

"I'll need that information to send the message, Mrs. Calhoun. Can you call your command ombudsman or another wife and find out? You must have a number around there somewhere. Then call me back, okay? I'll keep this message for you."

Caitlin hung up. She'd thought she was being so clever, but Pam was their ombudsman and Cait already knew her husband's command. She just didn't know… Unless this other Luke was somehow connected to her Luke's command.

Was he?

Aside from the wives' phone tree, the only other contact number she had was the OOD…. She dialed the duty desk for the Officer of the Day. Because of Luke's strict instructions, she'd never bothered his command once while he was alive.

"This is Caitlin Calhoun, Luke Calhoun's wife, er, widow." Would she ever get used to the idea of being a widow? She'd never even had the chance to get used to the idea of being a wife.

"Yes, Mrs. Calhoun," the Officer of the Day said with respect.

"This is going to sound odd, but is there another Luke Calhoun with the teams? Aside from my late husband, I mean."

"No, ma'am. We do have a couple Calhouns, though. But no other Luke Calhoun. Unless you mean Bruce?"

Bruce? Luke had never mentioned a Bruce.

"No," she said, disappointed. Of course it couldn't be that easy. Her eyes drifted to the stack of bills on the counter. "I have some mail here that I don't think belongs to my husband. It's addressed to a Luke Calhoun *Junior*." Well, now that was just a lie. She wished all those bills didn't belong to her husband. "I was wondering how I might track him down."

The man on the other end of the phone chuckled. "You mean Lucky. That's what you Calhouns get for having more than one Luke in the family." He cleared his throat, as if just realizing what he'd said. "Their mail gets mixed up all the time. Or at least it used to. We sure do miss Luke around here, Mrs. Calhoun. Is everything all right with you?"

Lucky?

She took a deep breath. "Yes," she lied. Did everyone except her know her husband had a brother?

"Just send the mail along to the command and I'll see that it gets forwarded."

Bingo. Speechless, she had to overcome her speech impediment *fast* before he hung up. "I'd…really like to forward it myself. See if I could put a stop to it. If you wouldn't mind, could you just give me his information?"

"Yeoman!" he shouted to someone. "There should be an emergency contact sheet on that desk somewhere for Bruce Calhoun. What unit is his brother with?"

Bruce again? Did Luke have more than one brother she didn't know about? Caitlin held her breath while she heard someone shuffling papers on the other end of the line.

"Yeah, here it is…. That's Master Sergeant Luke Calhoun Jr., USMC. Marine Expeditionary Unit One…" He rattled off the entire mailing address, e-mail address and cell-phone number while she scrambled for pen and paper to write it all down. She wound up using the back of an envelope of one of those bills she'd claimed were his.

Not a Navy SEAL. A Marine.

"Thank you," she managed as she hung up the phone. Preoccupied, she'd forgotten to ask for the other brother's information.

Pacing the living area of her apartment, which was only slightly bigger than the overstuffed storage unit she rented,

Caitlin nixed the idea of calling back the Red Cross. Not when she had all of his information right at her fingertips.

A "daddygram" might come as a bit of a shock.

So, should she write, call or e-mail the alleged father of her baby? Her brother-in-law. A complete stranger, no matter what his relationship to her husband.

She paced the length of her breakfast bar.

An e-mail would be quicker than a letter but not as personal. A phone call would be personal *and* quick. Or she might have to leave a message. Or he might be one of those soldiers who carried his cell phone into battle. She'd seen them on CNN, shooting with one hand while holding a phone up to an ear with the other.

In which case, e-mail would be the safer choice.

Either way, she'd wind up waiting for him to contact her....

And to think this morning she'd felt a little nauseous. How quickly her world had spun out of control.

The phone rang again.

"What?" she snapped into the receiver, fully expecting Pam to be on the other end of the line.

"Caitlin Calhoun?" That testosterone-laced voice did not belong to Pam. But it could very well belong to a guy shooting with one hand while talking with the other. There was a hint of something familiar that made her weak in the knees.

"Yes," she said, bracing herself. It could be just another bill collector. Why hadn't she checked the caller ID?

"You don't know me. Name's Lucky...Lucky Calhoun. I was wondering if CryoBank meant anything to—"

Caitlin hung up the phone.

CHAPTER TWO

"SMOOTH, LUCKY. REAL SMOOTH." He couldn't just punch Redial because he hadn't used his cell phone. It would have been too unreliable for this call. So he'd found a land line, one of the less used ones, and here he was punching in all those extra phone card numbers again. "Don't hang up," he said when she picked up this time.

"I won't." He could hear the raw emotion crackling over the line. Then silence. He could guess why she might be a little emotional.

He had twenty minutes left on his phone card, at best. He didn't know what to say, so he counted to ten, hoping it would come to him. Or that she'd feel compelled to fill the void. She didn't.

"Are you still there?" he asked.

Two F-18s roared overhead, one right after the other. He put a finger to his ear to hear her soft-spoken response in the other. "Yes."

"Are you okay?"

She hesitated. "No," she said through a broken sob.

Then the crying started in earnest. He'd never been very good with women who were criers. But as he looked around the airfield he didn't worry about what he was going to say next. He didn't have to ask if she was pregnant. Or if it was his. Those sobs told him everything he needed to know. "So I guess you have heard of CryoBank."

He heard her choke back a laugh. "Luke never even told me he had a brother."

"Half brother," he corrected. "We weren't that close." Now, *that* was an understatement. Which made him feel as if he had to say something more. "I'm sorry for your loss."

He hadn't taken emergency leave for the funeral—and not because the Marine Corps wouldn't let him. No, it ran much deeper than that.

It had taken him all of two seconds to put one and one together and come up with three. First the letter from Aunt Dottie saying the widow-bride wouldn't give up the flag or Little Luke's semen. And they were afraid she was going to do something stupid. "They" meaning Nora Jean, because he was pretty sure the rest of the family didn't give a damn what the widow did with her dead husband's sperm.

Then the letter from CryoBank. Or rather CryoBank's attorneys. The words *specimen* and *compromised* jumped out at him, along with a check. It was pretty self-explanatory.

Compromised. He snorted. In the military, *compromised* was a polite term for "screwed."

No, he didn't care what the widow did with her dead husband's sperm. But he did care what she did with his. "So, how pregnant are you?"

"*Pregnant!*" she snapped as another jet engine whistled overhead. "Is someone shooting at you?" She sniffed back her tears. The change in her demeanor rattled him. *Fear.* For him?

"No, I'm pretty safe right here," he lied. Safe was a relative term when standing next to a blast wall. "Those are our guys. But I don't have much time…. The pregnancy," he prompted. "How far along are you?"

He rephrased his question even though he didn't think he was being all that insensitive. Pregnant women were just overly sensitive. Or so he'd heard from more than one guy in the unit who'd left a pregnant wife behind.

"Three months."

That far. He dug at the ground with the toe of his boot. A little late to do anything about it now. Three whole months he'd been an expectant father and hadn't even known it. Hell, he didn't even know the mother. He might have imagined this conversation with one of any number of ex-girlfriends. But not with a total stranger.

"The baby's due in June."

The baby.

That soon.

"So what do we do about this?" he asked.

"This?" He heard confusion in her voice.

"Situation. CryoBank."

"I don't know."

That made two of them. "Just don't sign anything. I'm turning the whole matter over to JAG. Let the Navy and Marine Corps lawyers figure it out."

She didn't say anything for about a minute. At least that's what it felt like.

"You signed something? A release? A check?"

Another moment of silence.

A frustrated sigh escaped him. "I hope they offered you more than the thirty-five hundred dollars they offered me."

"Thirty-five *hundred?*"

"Should I feel insulted?" CryoBank was mistaken if they thought this a simple misappropriation of his semen.

"This really isn't your problem," she said.

"Then whose problem is it?" She was mistaken if she thought this wasn't his problem.

"I just meant I chose to have Luke's baby."

"Wrong Luke."

"I know this wasn't your choice. But if Luke and I had had trouble conceiving we might have asked you ourselves. A brother is a close DNA match and a brother-in-law a common sperm donor."

He doubted that. He really doubted that.

He and Luke were half brothers. But the only thing they had in common was the same name and the same father. And neither by choice. But he didn't bother correcting her.

"So I guess I'm asking…" She hesitated. "Could you see yourself as the donor?"

Donor. Scapegoat without the goat.

"And uncle," she added hastily. "It could be our little secret. No one else needs to know."

She didn't know what she was asking.

"Sounds like you've got this all figured out."

She'd given him an out, so why wasn't he taking it? What were his intentions when he'd picked up the phone? To tell her he was a stand-up guy? That he'd be there for her and the baby? He was. And he would be.

But he had hoped he was wrong about the whole sordid situation. He'd lived his entire life in Little Luke's shadow. And now this… "I'll think about it."

He heard a beep. The two-minute warning from his phone card. Twenty minutes up already?

"Please, promise me you'll keep this between us. Will you be back in the States anytime soon?" she asked. "Maybe it would be best if we discussed this in person."

Home. His tour of duty had been involuntarily extended, along with his enlistment in the Corps. So much for an all-volunteer force.

Seems he was out of choices these days.

A squadron of Black Hawk helicopters took off on the horizon. Search and destroy? Or search and rescue?

Another beep. One minute left for such an enormous decision.

"Are you still there?" she asked.

"Still here." Was it really fair to keep her hanging? As a Marine, war was his reality. Sometimes the question *what if* couldn't be avoided.

To hell with what he wanted. "A very involved uncle," he answered.

"Absolutely!"

"Look, I don't know when I'll get the chance to call again—"

"E-mail me—"

Click. Dial tone. *Damn.*

He didn't have her e-mail address.

CAITLIN SET THE PHONE BACK in its cradle. This time she hadn't been as eager for the connection to break. They'd left so much unsaid. She hadn't asked about the other brother. Brothers? And he hadn't told her when he'd be home.

Was San Diego even his home?

Camp Pendleton was a Marine base, wasn't it?

She shouldn't get so hung up on all the questions. He'd accepted his role. She didn't have it all figured out yet, but asking him to be her sperm donor was the solution.

Really, how involved would he be? He was a military man.

And he as much as admitted that they weren't a close family. He seemed more concerned with taking legal action against CryoBank than he was about her and the baby.

Caitlin put a comforting hand to her belly.

There was no need for her to feel this disappointed.

Their phone call had just reaffirmed what she'd known all along—that she was in this alone.

The important thing was that half brothers shared DNA.

This baby was Luke's no matter what.

And she'd keep telling herself that until she believed it. Because if she didn't, if she let the reality sink in, it would be like losing him all over again.

Caitlin was startled out of her reverie by pounding at the door.

That was either the landlady with December's bounced rent check, or it was Pam. A quick peek though the peephole and she could see, in keeping with the season, three wise women bearing gifts. Wiping her eyes, Caitlin answered the door.

"Why didn't you tell us what you were thinking so we could have talked you out of it?" Pam stepped past Caitlin, her arms full of what appeared to be maternity clothes.

"Maybe I didn't to be talked out of it."

"Of course you did." Pam dumped the clothes into Caitlin's arms. "Do you have any idea how hard it is to raise a child alone?"

"I'll manage. *You* manage." Caitlin tossed the bundle to the couch on top of her pillow and blanket. Her sleeping arrangements raised three pairs of eyebrows.

"He's not just gone, Caitlin. He's gone for good."

Everyone needed that one friend who would tell it to them like it was—for Caitlin, Pam was that friend. But she could be a little abrasive at times.

Caitlin prepared to square off with her now.

"She'll manage." Jill stepped in, handing over a small bag from The Holiday Store. And then there was that friend who was your cheerleader, no matter what. "We decided we couldn't wait for the wives' club meeting and our annual ornament exchange."

Caitlin had attended half a dozen of their weekly get-togethers, but only one since Luke's death because of how uncomfortable it made everyone. Including her.

"A little help here." Marilyn had wandered into the kitchenette to unpack two shopping bags full of carry-out containers from the Officer's Club. "I'll have you know I wouldn't go off my diet for just anyone. But we thought you could use some comfort food." She alternately waved and nibbled on a French fry. And then there was the friend who was so self-absorbed she made all your worries seem small.

"Open the bag," Jill encouraged.

Inside, Caitlin found an ornament for the tree she hadn't bothered to put up. The teddy bear had a rounded belly exposed under a T-shirt with the saying Baby On Board.

"Do you believe Jill actually had that T-shirt," Pam volunteered, plucking it from the pile of clothes to show it to her.

Caitlin didn't know whether to laugh or to cry.

"Wow," Jill said, "Luke's baby!"

"How does that whole frozen Popsicle thing work, anyway?" Marilyn, who didn't have children, wanted to know.

Pam cast the woman a warning glare, and Marilyn went back to stuffing her face with French fries. "We are happy for you, Caitlin," Pam tried to reassure her. "And we want you to know we're here for you."

An awkward silence followed. Caitlin's husband had been a junior officer in a world where women socialized according to their husband's rank.

And now she was a widow. A pregnant widow at that. No wonder they didn't know how to treat her anymore.

"But…" Caitlin prompted.

"No buts," Pam said, pushing aside the mound of clothes and guiding Caitlin to sit beside her on the couch. "The team is coming home for Christmas."

A longer, more awkward silence followed as Caitlin digested the news.

"We wanted to be the ones to tell you," Jill said.

"That's great," Caitlin stammered.

"Go ahead and cry, honey," Jill said sympathetically.

"No." Caitlin held back her tears. She really was happy for her friends. Their husbands were coming home. And in time for Christmas. "No, that's great," she repeated.

"We just found out today." Marilyn dusted the salt from her fingertips and deserted the fries with one last longing look.

"When?"

"Two days," Pam said.

Christmas Eve.

"I'll be there," Caitlin said in an overly bright voice.

Pam got that maternal look in her eye. The one Caitlin

imagined she gave her youngest when she was bandaging his boo-boos after a fall from his skateboard. "You know you don't have to."

"I want to."

Caitlin made it through lunch and an hour of polite conversation. She was a phony. She wasn't even a friend anymore. Not really. Not when she couldn't tell them the truth about her condition.

As soon as she closed the door on the wives Caitlin ran to the bathroom. She dug through the hamper for Luke's T-shirt. Pulling it over her head, over her clothes, she stuck her arms through the sleeves and sank to the tile floor.

She was pregnant. It wasn't her husband's baby.

And his team was coming home. Without him.

The dam burst.

AFTER WAITING IN THE INTERNET access lines for over an hour, Lucky checked his e-mail. Nothing from the widow-bride, not that he was expecting anything. He'd just spoken with her a few hours ago.

When Bruce appeared on his buddy list, Lucky sent his brother an Instant Message.

Lucky: what do you know about the widow-bride?
Bruce: not much, y
Lucky: do u have her sn?
Bruce: had his
Lucky: can you get hers?
Bruce: so you can bully the widow?
   i know you had reason to hate him, but i

    was just getting to know him
Lucky: no lecture
    i need her sn
Bruce: just tell me y
Lucky: i said so
Bruce: lol-BULLY
Lucky: I NEED IT!
Bruce: what message? will find way to pass
    it along
Lucky: FORGET IT!
Bruce: <signed off>

What about Bruce's allegiance to the brother he'd known all his life? It wasn't as if Bruce and Luke were ever going to be buddies. Officers and enlisted men didn't socialize. Hell, maybe SEALs did. But Bruce had been in Iraq while Luke was Stateside getting hitched. And as far as Lucky knew, he hadn't even gotten an invite to the wedding. So why was he being so protective of the widow-bride? Lucky pushed away from the computer more frustrated than ever.

"Internet dating's a bitch, ain't it?" Sergeant Jack Randall had been Lucky's spotter for the past four years. He was a good guy to have covering your six. But you didn't want him anywhere near your sweetheart or your sister. Not that Lucky had either. Which may have been why they got along so well.

"Someday those five fiancées of yours are going to be chatting with each other."

"Never happen," Randall said with the confidence of a man who had yet to be caught. "I've got it all figured out. I'm going to give each of them a different homecoming date. By the time I get bored with one I'll be moving on to another."

Cait had asked Lucky when he'd be home. He didn't have a definite date yet. He tried to imagine what it would be like to have someone waiting for him but couldn't.

"What if you don't get bored?"

Jack gave him a blank stare. "Guess I hadn't thought of that contingency. You ever not get bored?"

"No," Lucky answered honestly. "But maybe it's because we pick the wrong women." Lucky had signed up with half a dozen different Internet dating services over his four tours in Iraq. He just didn't find it as addictive as some of the guys in his unit did.

He preferred picking up women the old-fashioned way, in bars. Better that than finding out your cyber squeeze was really some three-hundred-pound guy in a bathrobe with way too much time on his hands.

But with no pick-up bars in sight, that left the Internet. He'd never had to lie to a woman online because he'd never let it get that personal. He didn't make promises lightly, and never ones he couldn't keep.

Please, promise me you'll keep this between us. He barely knew her, yet here he was guarding the biggest secret of his life.

"How can you afford all those engagement rings?" Lucky asked, thinking of one diamond-and-emerald ring in particular. That was some token Luke had given Cait.

"Combat pay."

"You forget I know just how little you make."

"Cubic zirconia."

"Fake diamonds?"

Randall shrugged. "Costs $29.99 plus shipping and handling. Available online."

Lucky shook his head. "You get a gal to fall for that, then you're both getting what you deserve." Okay, so no gal deserved to be stuck with Randall. Least of all one so blinded by love and cubic zirconia she couldn't imagine he'd cheat her out of the real thing.

This cost comparison got him thinking about the kind of price tag he'd put on love. Probably the industry standard of two and a half times his monthly base pay. He was more practical than romantic. Which explained why he was still single at thirty-two.

The Marine Corps didn't issue brides with their seabags.

Kids, either.

"Look her up on Google."

"What?"

Randall nodded toward Lucky's computer screen. "Look her up on Google."

Lucky wasn't a cyber geek, but he wasn't a cyber idiot, either. He'd found Cait's phone number and address online. He just hadn't thought to research her on the Internet.

Taking the advice of a master, Lucky looked up Caitlin Calhoun and came up with 1,204 useless bits and pieces of information: her physical address and phone number—both of which he already had—and one site with potential, a photography studio in Annapolis, Maryland.

He clicked on the link and came face-to-face with Caitlin and Luke's online wedding album. Yeah, like he really needed to see them feeding each other cake. It was just as well he didn't have the necessary password to check out the rest of the photo shoot.

The beautiful bride. The handsome naval officer.

It was enough to make him want to puke.

The last time he'd seen Luke in those choker whites was at his brothers', as in brothers' plural, graduation from Basic Underwater Demolition/SEAL training. He'd managed to avoid Luke for most of the formalities and the reception that followed.

They'd crossed paths in the parking lot afterward.

Lucky had raised the middle-finger salute. Two of Luke's men had tried to tear into him for that show of insubordination. After all, he was an enlisted Marine, and Luke had been a naval officer. But Luke had held them back. "It's okay. My big brother's just being his asshole self."

Big brother.

They'd let it drop as a family matter. If another officer had been present, Lucky would have been in some serious shit.

Luke could have gotten him into trouble.

So why hadn't he?

But Lucky already knew the answer.

Luke had had no reason to envy Lucky the way Lucky had envied his half brother. Because Luke had had it all. And when Lucky looked at that wedding photo, he had all the more reason to be jealous. Caitlin Calhoun wasn't just beautiful, she was breathtaking.

Blond hair, done up. Brown eyes that sparkled. And a smile that held nothing back.

Her groom—his little brother—must have been itching under his choker collar to get her out of that sexy-virgin wedding gown.

Lucky wracked his brain for the word used to describe brides and pregnant woman. *Radiant.*

Caitlin Calhoun was radiant in her love for her husband.

Lucky shifted uncomfortably in his seat.

What made a woman, even one so obviously in love, want to have her dead husband's baby?

He couldn't even begin to answer that question. As lucky as he was, he'd never found that kind of love.

Ironically, he located her e-mail address at the bottom of the page—a way to contact the bride and groom to get the photo album password. He clicked on the address hyperlink and found himself staring at white space, his mind as blank as the screen.

What was he supposed to say to a woman who'd asked him to be her sperm donor after the fact? Lucky scrubbed a tired hand over the day's growth of stubble. It wasn't as if she'd planned it. She was the real victim in this. But that didn't make him feel any less helpless. He still had to speak with a JAG officer about his will and survivors' benefits before he could get any sleep tonight.

No telling how long that would take.

Another line. Another couple of hours.

He double-clicked on Caitlin's e-mail address and changed it to Bruce's.

Subj: The Widow-Bride
Date: Saturday, December 22, 2007 11:52:07 p.m.
From: LuckyStrikes@scoutsniper.mil
To: B_Calhoun@marinerecruiter.mil

If anything happens to me, take care of the widow-bride. That's an order, Marine.

Lucky

"Sarg!" Tick burst in. "Captain wants you to round up the squad. We're moving out."

Lucky hit Send before he could think twice about it.

Bruce had way too much time on his hands now that he was out of the hospital. The last thing Lucky needed was his brother hooking up with the pregnant widow-bride. Now there was another Calhoun family happy ending just waiting to happen. But Bruce had his own reasons for staying away from Caitlin Calhoun, and Lucky needed someone he could trust.

CAITLIN DROPPED HER BUTT DOWN on the couch, clutching a bowl of oatmeal-raisin cookie dough to her chest. She'd been up all night baking cookies. Or rather, she'd baked cookies all night because she was up, letting her wedding DVD play over and over again.

The team was coming home today.

She wanted to be there. She needed to be.

She'd even bought a new dress. Black with tiny red rose-buds—a maternity/mourning/homecoming dress, if there was such a thing.

She'd braved the crowded mall full of last-minute holiday shoppers. Then made it up to the check-out counter at Macy's with an armful of maternity clothes off the sales racks…only to face the embarrassment of having her debit card declined.

She had hoped to balance out her friends' hand-me-downs with a few newer pieces. But because of the five-day bank hold on the CryoBank check and the seven- to ten-day wait on her replacement credit cards, she'd had to put everything back. Everything except that dress—which wasn't on sale—and which she paid for with her limited cash.

How desperate was she that she'd left the tag on so she'd have the option of taking it back? She really couldn't afford it.

But she wanted to look her best today.

That wasn't going to happen. Her hair was as limp as the rest of her felt. Her eyes were puffy from lack of sleep and red-rimmed from crying. And her smile had flat-lined the day Luke's heart had stopped beating.

No, his heart was here, beating inside her.

Luke's baby.

Wrong Luke. She heard that arrogant voice as clearly as if he were standing behind her, whispering it in her ear. She didn't know when she'd decided he was the enemy. None of this was his fault. But he made a convenient scapegoat.

Two days. And no e-mail.

She didn't know whether to think of *him* as Luke or Lucky. Both names were problematic for her. Luke for obvious reasons. And Lucky because… Well, what grown man went by the name of Lucky?

The truth was, she couldn't stop thinking about him.

He was her living, breathing connection to Luke.

But she didn't want to think about him. And she didn't want to think about what two days and no e-mail might mean.

After several more minutes crying into her cookie dough, Caitlin put it aside to get dressed for homecoming. Was an e-mail really too much to ask?

AN HOUR LATER CAITLIN WAS standing in a packed airplane hangar at Naval Air Station, North Island. The place was filled with red, white and blue helium balloons and Christmas decorations. And anticipation. Santa wore combat boots and looked as if he'd be equally comfortable toting an M-16, instead of a bag of toys.

Parents, wives and children of all ages waved homemade banners welcoming their SEAL team home. When the C-130 touched down, the overhead speakers blasted out music.

Caitlin felt like the only one not celebrating with Kool & the Gang. She stood off to the side of the milling crowd, an observer to the joyful and tearful reunions as the men deplaned.

To her right—two pairs of boots, two rifles, two helmets. Two men who would not be coming home.

They already had—in body bags and flag-draped coffins.

The Zahn family wasn't there. The sister was active-duty military. And the parents either weren't living, or lived in another state.

The widow-bride stood alone.

Following a brief welcome-home speech, the commanding officer offered Caitlin his personal condolences. "On behalf of a grateful nation, the President of the United States and a proud Navy…"

Caitlin tried to draw comfort from the sentiment as she had at Luke's interment.

Though the Navy had been well represented, none of these men had been there. She knew them only through their wives and Luke's letters. But the sincerity of his teammates meant the world to her as they took time out of their own lives to pay their respects.

As word spread of her pregnancy, she had her stomach rubbed for luck more times than a jade Buddha.

Her cheeks flamed bright red. They believed this baby was

Luke's. And that she was some kind of hero for having her deceased husband's baby. She wished she could believe it, too.

More than once she thought she caught sight of Luke in the crowd. She had to remind herself that Luke was dead. Besides, this figment of her imagination was wearing a Marine uniform. Guilty conscience.

"Calhoun!" someone called.

Caitlin swiveled around, catching sight of an enlisted man, and following him through the press of bodies. "Calhoun!" he called again. "Wait up!"

This time an enlisted Marine, hobbled by crutches from what she could see of his head and shoulders, stopped and waited for the other man. The Marine looked enough like Luke to be his...*brother*.

He hadn't deplaned with the rest of them. Had he been here all along? Somewhere in the crowd? Her heart raced. Why, with all the attention she was getting, hadn't he introduced himself?

The two men neared an exit, and by the time Caitlin got there, they were gone. She stepped outside into the bright Southern California sunshine. The area was deserted. Disappointed, she turned to go back inside and almost mowed down a man coming out.

"Did you see that enlisted man? He was calling to someone," she said. "Do you know who it was?"

"You mean Bruce, Mrs. Calhoun, your brother-in-law?"

CHAPTER THREE

"MRS. CALHOUN. MRS. CALHOUN!" Caitlin's landlady charged up the terrace steps after her. Tucking her mail and the gift from Luke's aunt inside her purse, Caitlin waited outside her third-floor apartment for her landlady to catch up. Someone had left a fruit basket outside her door. Caitlin bent to retrieve the card.

To Mrs. Calhoun. From the Team.

When had she stopped being Caitlin Calhoun and become this whole other person, this widow, Mrs. Calhoun? Caitlin could count on one hand the number of times she'd been called *Mrs.* while Luke had been alive.

The first had been at their wedding reception—their first dance as husband and wife—*"Ladies and gentlemen, Lieutenant and Mrs. Luke Calhoun."* And then again on the flight to the U.S. Virgin Islands, and while checking into the Ritz-Carlton on St. Thomas.

And the following morning, a sleepy-eyed Luke had awakened her with a kiss and a *"Good morning, Mrs. Calhoun."*

When they'd returned from their honeymoon, the first thing they'd done was get her a military dependant I.D. card with her married name. By the end of the week, she'd stood in lines on and off base.

Housing. Security. The DMV. The Navy Federal Credit Union.

Until the transformation was complete.

She was Caitlin Calhoun.

Mrs. Luke Calhoun. Mrs. Calhoun.

Except she didn't know who that person was anymore. Maybe she'd never known. Her future, her dreams, were full of uncertainty. And if she heard one more *Mrs. Calhoun* in that patronizing tone she was going to scream.

"Mrs. Calhoun!"

Caitlin bit her tongue and turned to face Mrs. Pèna, who'd stopped one step shy of the top. The woman's angry color and heaving bosom could be attributed to the climb or to the fact that the stalwart Filipino was missing her afternoon soap.

"Just a few more days. Please, Mrs. Pèna," Caitlin pleaded. After paying her rent two weeks late, the check had bounced. Three business days left on that five-day hold, and Caitlin was counting down every one of them.

"Your brother-in-law already paid December's rent."

"My what?" She'd spent an exhausting afternoon trying to track him down and now her landlady was telling her he'd been here and paid her rent? Caitlin stood with her mouth gaping.

"That's what I thought." Mrs. Pèna waggled her finger. "Widow or no widow, no monkey business in the apartment or I throw you out!" The woman descended the steps, muttering something about military men being bad for a widow's reputation. "And don't be late with January's rent!" she tossed back over her shoulder.

After leaving the Naval Air Station, Caitlin had stopped by

the post office to pick up a package. Her aunt by marriage had sent her a pair of slipper socks knitted out of flashy-colored fun fur. And then she'd gone on a wild-goose chase to follow his aunt's instruction, to deliver a similar package to the amputee ward at Balboa Naval Hospital. That's where Caitlin had discovered her brother-in-law, Bruce, was no longer an in-patient, but an outpatient.

It was just as well the trail had ended there. After the way he'd avoided her today she didn't feel comfortable leaving what she suspected were a pair of slipper socks for an amputee she'd never met.

She would have liked to have met him, though.

"Mrs. Pèna," Caitlin called down to the courtyard. "Did he say anything else?"

"Yes." Mrs. Pèna stopped outside her own apartment door. "He said to wish you a Merry Christmas, Mrs. Calhoun."

LUCKY STOOD in the chow line, in full battle dress, for his first hot meal in two days. The next twenty-four hours couldn't come and go fast enough. Fighting escalated in every region during holy days, no matter the religion.

"Did you know she was pregnant?" Was that censure in his brother's tone, or a bad connection?

"Yeah," he admitted into his cell phone as the mess specialist slopped scrambled eggs onto his plate. Instead of Midnight Mass, he was celebrating Christmas Eve with midnight rations at the Coalition Café.

"With Luke's baby?" his brother continued.

Lucky pushed his tray down the line and slid into the first available seat. He knew better than to attribute the sudden pang in his gut to hunger. He wasn't all that hungry anymore. "So I've been told."

"I guess that explains your e-mail."

"I guess it does."

"Like hell it does! *Take care of the widow-bride?*" Now *that* was censure. "Since when do you give a damn about Luke's wife?"

"Widow," he corrected. "She's Luke's widow, not his wife." The lack of sleep showed in his irritation. "And for the record, I changed my will this morning." Bruce was the executor of his estate, not that he had an estate. But he did have some money saved. "I'm leaving everything to Caitlin and the baby."

"*Caitlin?* Since when do you call the widow-bride by name? Two nights ago you didn't even know her e-mail address."

Lucky salted his eggs with unnecessary vigor. "If you called to give me shit, you can quit wasting my cell-phone minutes."

"Finally, something you've said that makes sense. I just thought you'd want to know she's in trouble."

"What kind of trouble?" The shaker stilled in his hand.

"Money trouble."

Lucky put the shaker down and shoveled his first mouthful of salted egg, then stabbed a wedge of pancake to push it down. Luke had been an officer, making more than what Lucky made; he should have had money in the bank. And even if he didn't, there were survivors' benefits. Luke's pension. Social Security. Her settlement with CryoBank…

Not to mention she came from old money.

She should never have to work a day in her life.

Unless she wanted to.

"That doesn't make any sense," he said around a mouthful.

"Her mailbox was overstuffed with bills. And there was an eviction notice posted on her door. I paid December's rent and I can hit up the guys on the team for January's, but…" there was a long pause "…she was Luke's wife. I think we should ask Big Luke for help."

Lucky's mouthful of syrup-soaked pancakes turned as dry as the dust kicked up by a convoy of Humvees. He'd never asked Big Luke for anything in his life, and he wasn't about to start now. "I'll take care of the widow-bride. How much is her rent?"

"Eighteen-fifty."

When Bruce named the staggering amount, Lucky felt as if he'd swallowed sand. "Beachfront?"

"Oceanview. Coronado."

He pushed the food around on his plate. If it was an ocean-view she wanted why couldn't she have found a place in Imperial Beach? He didn't know the extent of her money woes, but stress couldn't be good for the baby. "How'd she look?"

"You just volunteered what amounts to half your base pay and all you have to say is, how'd she look?"

"Well?"

"Well what?"

"Is she showing?"

"Showing? Yeah…no…I don't know."

"Radiant?"

"Who are you and what have you done with my big brother? You do realize you're obsessed with a woman you've never met?"

"I'm not obsessed."

And if he was he had every reason to be.

"How'd you find out about the baby?" Bruce asked.

"You know Dottie…" Lucky answered evasively.

"I know you must be her favorite nephew."

"Dottie doesn't play favorites. She'll knit us both a pair of slipper socks for Christmas."

"My point exactly."

Open mouth, insert foot. Lucky hadn't been thinking about his brother's amputated leg. But he was probably right about Aunt Dottie knitting them both slipper socks. "She means well."

"Dottie didn't know about the baby."

Lucky winced. "What'd you tell her?"

"I didn't know it was some big secret. The whole team knows the widow-bride went to CryoBank. What I don't know is how you knew before anyone else. You're still in Iraq, for crying out loud."

Lucky held his peace. He'd made Cait a promise.

"Just tell me your sudden interest in the widow-bride has nothing to do with Luke," Bruce finally said. "This isn't some twisted form of revenge…is it?"

Twisted maybe, revenge no.

"My interest in Cait is my business."

"Cait, now, is it? Then for the record… She's not just radiant, she's smoking-hot. She's also our brother's pregnant widow. And he was head-over-heels in love with her. You step out of line and you're going to have a whole team of Navy SEALs breathing down your leather neck."

"Is that a threat?"

"Just good advice."

"Yeah, well, you and your bottom-feeder Navy buddies stay away from that heat."

"I'm not the one looking to get burned."

CAITLIN BURNED ANOTHER BATCH of cookies. She shouldered the phone while she used a broom handle to knock off the smoke alarm. Her midnight confession to her mother-in-law was not going as planned.

"You're what?" Nora Jean's shock reverberated long-distance.

"Baking," she repeated, setting the broom aside to pull on her lobster-claw oven mitt. She'd found an outlet for her late-night baking, an entire ward of kindred spirits who all knew something about loss. Whatever cookies she didn't pack off to her brothers-in-law she intended to bring back to the hospital amputee ward.

She waved away the smoke. Reaching into the oven, she pulled out two charred cookie sheets, one at a time, and set them on top of the stove. Then she tossed off the mitt for a better grip on the phone.

Tonight her mother-in-law loved her.

Grief had made her mother-in-law irrational at times. At least they had that much in common. Caitlin wouldn't know a rational thought from an irrational one. And couldn't trust her own decisions.

Late-night shadows danced across the walls. Caitlin's attention strayed to the bright contrast of the TV screen and her muted wedding DVD, where everything was white.

White uniform. White cake. White dress.

"Caitlin, come to Colorado for a visit," Nora Jean urged. "I shouldn't be alone for the holidays in my condition."

Her condition? If my mother-in-law only knew.

"I'll even splurge for the ticket. It'll be waiting for you at the airport."

White Christmas.

She'd missed her chance to take her father up on a similar offer to go to Maryland. "I can't." Her hand strayed to her midriff. Her hand was doing a lot of that these days. "A retail opportunity has presented itself," she said, mimicking the staffer from the temp agency.

"You have a job?"

Why did the woman sound so surprised? It wasn't as if she was incapable of supporting herself. Or of baking.

"It's temporary. Just like the last one. Christmas through New Year's." If she was lucky. She needed the income.

She'd had a job shortly after arriving in San Diego. In fact, she'd received several offers after passing the state board and licensing exam. Then Luke had been killed and she'd quit working, with the intention of moving back home and working in her father's drugstore.

So here she was, back at square one.

She'd signed on with a temp agency to keep afloat and to buy herself some time. But for the life of her she didn't know what she was waiting to decide. Luke wasn't coming back. No matter how much she wanted him to.

"So you're working Christmas?" Nora Jean sighed. "Did you at least get the fruitcake I sent you?"

"Yes, thank you."

Nora Jean must have really hated her that day. Caitlin hated fruitcake.

Caitlin had sent her mother-in-law a memory box she'd

bought from the Navy Exchange. A simple velvet-lined, wooden box with a raised United States Navy seal on top. She'd put a lock of Luke's hair inside. She'd snipped it the morning he'd left, while he was still sleeping.

She could still remember the look on his face when he'd woken up to find her hovering over him with a pair of scissors. She'd put that stolen lock to her lip in a mock mustache, and he'd started laughing. Then he'd tickled her until she'd begged for mercy.

That was a good memory. Except her laughter had turned to tears when it came time to say goodbye. She'd prolonged that last kiss to the last possible moment. She just hadn't realized at the time it really was their last kiss.

While Luke's mother continued talking, Caitlin toyed with the ornament from Jill and the wives that was sitting on her kitchen counter. That would be the last she'd see or hear from her friends for a while. With their husbands home they had other plans for the holidays. And who could blame them?

"…I worry that you're not eating properly," her mother-in-law said, and Caitlin realized she'd missed most of the conversation.

"I'm eating," she defended herself, thinking of the oatmeal-raisin cookie dough. With a guilty glance toward the untouched fruit basket from the team, she vowed to do a better job.

"Did I mention I've lost twenty pounds?"

As if the amount of weight lost were an indicator of who loved Luke more. Why did the woman persist on making everything a competition?

They both loved him. "Nora, I have to go."

"The offer stands. Think about it, at least."

And then there was a side to Nora Jean that could be so sweet, tempting Caitlin with an offer like that. "I will...I promise."

White lie.

The job offer wasn't the only reason she couldn't go. Her mother-in-law would realize she'd put on a few pounds. And she would have to tell her.

And defend her decision.

Ultimately, it would all come down to a little white lie when she looked the woman in the eye and told her she was carrying Luke's baby. Well, not a lie exactly.

She *was* carrying Luke's baby.

Wrong Luke.

That was the problem with keeping secrets. She had no one to talk to. The one person who shared her secret was a million miles away.

"*Mom,*" she said, trying to soften the blow with the endearment, "there's something I have to tell you..."

"I'VE NEVER BEEN WITH A WOMAN," Tick confessed.

Merry Christmas. Lucky saw real fear in the kid's eyes. They were trapped in a stairwell when they should have been making their way up. Close-quarters combat was not the optimal employment of a sniper team. Three of their four rifles were bolt-action, not automatic.

The kid was too terrified to move.

"I'm not your priest. Keep your head down. And keep moving, Marine." As his sergeant, it was Lucky's job to be tough on the kid.

Lucky used their only automatic weapon to provide cover fire as he shoved Tick past the gaping hole left minutes ago by a rocket-propelled grenade. Eddie Estes pulled the kid to safety as insurgents returned fire from across the alley.

Lucky sank back against what was left of the sandstone wall, breathing heavily after four flights of fighting; cordite and copper burned his nostrils. The copper was his own blood.

Four tours without a scratch, and here he was bucking for a Purple Heart. But what really pissed him off—the shrapnel had cut through a perfectly good tattoo. How lucky could a guy get?

One more floor and they'd have the advantage of the rooftop. Welcome to the Ramada Inn. The typical rooftop in Ramandi was surrounded by a four-foot wall, sandbagged for sniping and to protect against mortar rounds. In the streets below, a pinned-down company of fellow Marines were counting on them.

Higher ground.

One more floor.

"You want to hear my confession?" Randall asked, sidling up next to him.

"It'd be a hell of a lot more interesting."

Lucky nodded once to Randall, then opened a barrage of bullets as the spotter rolled to the other side. Another barrage and Lucky dove after him. The four of them scrambled up another flight of stairs.

Last landing. Bigger hole.

They'd be exposed those last few steps to the roof.

"Anything you'd care to confess?" Randall asked, eyeing the opening.

"Nope." Lucky grit his teeth and ignored the blood trickling down his arm. It was just a scratch.

"You need stitches," Tick said. "You want me to call the

corpsman? Because I could call the corpsman." The kid reached for his mic.

"It's nothing," Lucky grunted in his best John Wayne.

Sergeant Stryker, now there was a Marine. *Sands of Iwo Jima.* Best damn movie ever made.

He didn't need some kid telling him he was bleeding. And he didn't need a corpsman risking his neck for a few stitches when there were Marines dying in the streets.

"I was slapped with a three-thousand yard restraining order while on leave," Estes spoke up to deflect Lucky's wrath.

"Don't you mean three hundred feet?" Lucky said with a measure of disbelief.

"Not after she told the judge I was a Marine sniper. I can't go near a bell tower, clock tower, water tower or rooftop in my hometown."

"What the hell did you do?"

"Rang a bell." At Lucky's expression of disbelief, Estes shrugged. "From the church bell tower. During her wedding rehearsal to another guy."

"Did she still marry that other guy?" Tick wanted to know.

"Didn't stick around long enough to find out," Estes said matter-of-factly.

"I bought a real diamond." Randall sounded resigned. Whether that was to marriage or the other big unknown, Lucky didn't know. The thing was they all had unfinished business.

His team looked at him expectantly. They were counting on him to get them out of this mess. So he had to give them something.

"I keep a copy of *What To Expect When You're Expecting* under my rack," he said, resigned to nothing, except that last flight of stairs.

CAITLIN TRUDGED UP THE LAST few steps to her apartment. She wasn't used to standing all day. And those extra five pounds she carried around in baby weight felt like twenty to her aching back and feet. Not to mention she was carrying a bag of groceries in each hand.

Okay, ten pounds. Without the groceries.

But they still felt like twenty.

Once inside, she put away her groceries, popped a Lean Cuisine into the microwave and grabbed a Yoplait from the fridge for dessert, which she ate first. It was Christmas dinner, after all. She could eat her dessert first.

She screened her phone messages between spoonfuls of strawberry-banana yogurt. Twelve in eight hours. That was a new record even for Nora Jean.

She'd told her mother-in-law about the baby last night—omitting the part about the sperm mix-up. Couples used donor sperm all the time. How was this any different?

Her commitment to Luke was real. If she confessed everything to her father right now, he'd understand. But somehow she didn't think that argument would hold up against a mother-in-law who'd lost her only son.

Caitlin certainly wasn't ready for that conversation.

But message number thirteen was Nora Jean again.

How lucky could a girl get?

LUCKY PUSHED ASIDE THE TENT flap. He glanced at the mail on his rack. The package from his aunt barely registered. Like every man in his squad his gaze drifted to Tick's empty rack.

"The dumbshit kid!" Eddie Estes screamed. "I told him

to keep his head down." Estes sat on his rack and bawled like a baby.

There were murmurs of sympathy, but there was no consoling Estes. Not if you wanted to keep your teeth in your mouth instead of in a glass of Polident by your bed.

Lucky sat on his own rack and went through the motions of stowing his rifle. He ignored Dottie's package. And his mail.

Estes shouted obscenities at someone who had the misfortune of wandering into the tent. Lucky tucked his mail away to deal with the sergeant. Two of the guys reached Estes first and held him back. The young Marine corporal who stood just inside the tent flap held an empty file box. "I need to get his things," he tried to explain.

"You're not touching his stuff with your filthy hands—"

"Hey," Lucky warned Estes. "You're out of line."

"Dirty Hands" tagged 'em and bagged 'em. "Clean Hands" logged personal effects. Unenviable jobs at best.

All the honor went to the military escort—the "Blue Bark."

He'd send Estes home with the body. The sergeant was in no condition to carry on here, but he might be of some comfort to the family. Estes had loved Tick like a little brother—they all had.

"We've got it," Lucky said, taking the file box from Corporal Clean Hands, who made a hasty retreat. "Snap out of it, Marine," he ordered Estes. "Let's get this over with."

They spent the next several minutes going through Tick's footlocker. Laughing at the stupid stuff Richard "Tick" Tanner III used to say—it was either that or cry.

They'd made it up to the roof and back down again. Lucky had even let the corpsman stitch him up on the ride back in the Humvee.

Then their convoy had been hit.

Thirteen times Lucky had been in an armored Humvee when he'd heard that unmistakable pop. Thirteen times he'd survived a roadside bomb. It wasn't the IED—Improvised Explosive Device—that had killed Tick. They'd lost him in the ambush that had followed. A battle that had lasted less than an hour, but in the end Tick was gone.

"Polish up your brass," Lucky said when they were done, as a way of informing Estes of his decision to let him go.

"What about this?" Estes unfolded a letter tucked into the corner of Tick's footlocker.

Lucky took the letter and read it, even though he was familiar with every life-altering word.

Please take a moment to consider your future family dreams....

The kid had counted on him to make his decisions for him. The right decisions. Lucky couldn't choose who lived or died in battle. Only, he couldn't shake the feeling that when it came to CryoBank he'd let Tick down.

Lucky replayed that day over in his head.

Tick stretched out on his cot. Estes beaning the kid with a can of Pringles. Tick playing the *what if* game.

What if this was it?

For Tick, it was.

Lucky could pay the storage fees and let the family decide. But they might make the wrong decision. And he knew what Tick would have wanted.

The same thing Lucky would want if someone put that same piece of paper in front of him today.

Life. A legacy.

Something that said he mattered to this world.

Lucky took out his nubby pencil, the one he always carried on patrol. He put his X on the line.

$\boxed{X}$ *Donate my specimen.*

Eddie looked taken aback for a moment. "Yeah, yeah," he finally agreed. "Do you mind if I write a letter to go with this? You never know, his kid might want to know something about him someday."

"I think he'd like that. Just don't write about what a dumbshit he was."

Estes chuckled. "I'll stick to the truth. He was a guy with a lot left to learn. And he was too young to die."

LUCKY LEFT THEIR TENT AFTER that. He made it around the corner before stopping to puke his guts out. Ten square miles of tents later, he still couldn't get that concrete-slab mortuary out of his mind. Four boxcar-sized camouflaged refrigerators held remains until they could be sent home.

But on that slab every body cavity was searched for unexploded ordnance by some guy they wouldn't even sit next to in the chow hall. Too superstitious.

Who knows, maybe it was "the hands" who wouldn't eat with them. It couldn't be easy. It had never been easy for Lucky. In fact, it was a hell of a lot easier not to form any attachments at all.

There was something about losing Tick that hit a little too close to home. Like any kid brother, Tick was so annoying you wanted him out of your hair, but when he was gone—really gone—you missed him.

And somehow you knew you were never going to be the same. Kind of the way he'd felt the night the chaplain had taken him to see Luke's body. Hands that never trembled, trembled just thinking about it now.

He'd put so much time and effort into hating Luke, he'd forgotten that it wasn't really Luke he hated. He'd never taken the chance to get to know his half brother and now he never would. He envied Bruce that. The chaplain had seemed surprised when Lucky had refused the honor of escorting the body home.

There was no honor in his shame.

At the end of the line for Luke there'd have been Nora Jean and Big Luke. Lucky couldn't have dealt with their grief when he could barely come to terms with his own. But, he realized now, there would have been someone else at the airport to collect the body.

The widow-bride. Heartbroken. Trying to be strong.

Much like she'd sounded on the phone the other day. He couldn't change what had happened with CryoBank. But he could put aside his feelings and see her through this. He owed Luke that much at least.

Finding a quiet place, or as quiet as a military base could be operating 24/7 in a war zone, he pulled out his cell phone. This call was going to cost him an arm and a leg. It was worth every appendage just to know she was all right.

"Merry Christmas," he said when she picked up, even though for him Christmas had come and gone. "Were you asleep?"

"Yes," she answered groggily.

He should have realized she would be asleep. Baghdad was ten hours ahead of San Diego. He could hear her sitting up in bed, or maybe he was just imagining it.

"What time is it?" she asked.

"Early or late. Depending on how you look at it."

"Well, by my clock it's late, 11:59 p.m. Do you leave all your Christmas calls for the last minute, Calhoun? I've been worried sick about you. You were supposed to e-mail me. Are you okay?"

"I'm sorry." He wasn't about to tell a young widow that he wasn't okay. He'd lost a man today. A boy barely nineteen whose parents would always remember Christmas Day as the day their son had died. Or that he'd needed to call her, to hear her, to be reassured by her that a part of him would go on even though he might not make it.

"Don't be sorry," she said. "Just be okay."

How many days ago had it been since his life had changed? Three? Four? But he—hell, *she,* knew better than most that life could change in an instant. "Are *you* okay?"

"I'm fine."

"The baby…"

"*We're* fine. I could send you the ultrasound if you'd like to see for yourself."

"I'd like that."

"Ohmigod—"

"What?" he demanded, ready to leap through the phone line to her rescue.

"I just felt a flutter."

"A flutter?" He barely disguised his awe as he tried to

imagine what a *flutter* felt like. "Isn't it a little soon?" he asked, thinking of the book under his bed. Quickening could occur between weeks fourteen and twenty-six. Earlier for smaller women.

"The doctor said I'd start to feel movement anytime. If you hadn't called…I'd have slept right through it. Calhoun, you just gave me the best Christmas present ever."

"Glad to be of service." He chuckled at the excitement in her voice. "What else did the doc say? Boy or girl?"

"I don't know the sex."

He'd kind of like to know. Not that it mattered. "Ten fingers. Ten toes. As long as he's healthy, right?" He gave the stock answer he'd heard from other expectant fathers.

"*He?*" She laughed at his slipup. "I'd kind of like a boy, too."

The amazing thing was that he wanted this baby at all. She was the one who had given him a gift. "Thank you."

"For what?" she asked behind a yawn.

He'd almost forgotten she was in bed. And probably had to get up. Maybe go to work in a few hours. Was she working? He was amazed by how little he actually knew about her. Keeping her on the line was selfish. He just couldn't bring himself to hang up yet. "Just thank you."

"You haven't even gotten the cookies yet."

"You sent me cookies?"

"Well, not yet. But I baked them and as soon as the post office opens I'm there. I hope you like chocolate chip because I ate all the oatmeal-raisin cookie dough."

"I love chocolate chip."

He loved the idea that she'd baked for him.

"They were Luke's favorite, too."

He'd almost made it through the entire conversation believing it was just the two of them. That would be a futile fantasy at best.

Cait wasn't his wife. She was Luke's widow.

Her phone demeanor changed after she mentioned Luke. "Do you think it unforgivable to keep a secret, even if keeping that secret makes someone happy?"

"That depends," he answered carefully.

"I told Nora Jean about the baby," she said, her voice quiet. "I didn't tell her about your part in this."

"I see." It's what he'd agreed to. And when the child was born he'd look like a Calhoun. Because he'd be a Calhoun. If he was going to do right by Cait, he had to stop thinking of this baby as his.

"It seems unforgivable now. But she was so happy, I just couldn't…"

"Cait, you don't owe Nora Jean an explanation. You don't owe anyone anything." Least of all him.

"Maybe not," she agreed, but changed the subject just the same. "When will you be home? We can't wait to meet you."

His heart almost stopped beating right then and there. "A couple of months. Before the baby's due."

If his luck held.

"Promise?"

"I can't promise."

"Luke would never make me that promise. Maybe if he had—"

"Cait, it doesn't work that way."

"What if I need to hear it?"

Then he needed to say it. As if wanting something that bad made it so. "I promise."

CHAPTER FOUR

THREE MONTHS LATER he kept his word.

The unit boarded a chartered commercial flight out of Baghdad. The atmosphere on the Boeing 747 was jubilant, despite the number of flag-draped caskets in the cargo hold.

The plane wasn't on the ground long. The added threat of RPGs—rocket-propelled grenades—made landings and take-offs especially dangerous.

Lucky held his breath during takeoff and didn't let it out again until they were in the air.

Butterflies. That's what a flutter kick felt like. A stomach full of butterflies. As of their latest phone call, the baby was trying out for in utero soccer.

Lucky had just settled into his coach seat next to Randall when a female flight attendant, carrying a flute of champagne, approached him. "The captain would like to seat you in first class."

"Oh," he started to protest, "I'm not—"

"Go on." Randall gave him a shove.

The flight attendant handed him the champagne, and Lucky grabbed his carry-on and followed the best pair of legs he'd seen in ten months as cheers and jeers followed him up the aisle.

First class was reserved for officers and new fathers. The new fathers would be allowed to deplane first.

"Saved you a seat." Captain George patted the one next to his. "About to become an uncle," the captain explained to the flight attendant. "Baby's daddy was killed in Iraq."

The attendant said something appropriately sympathetic, made sure he stowed his carry-on and buckled in, then left to see to the rest of her first-class passengers.

His butterflies started up again. Lucky sipped from the flute in his hand, which did nothing to settle his stomach. He'd guarded Cait's secret well. His entire unit believed he was his baby's uncle.

They refueled in Kuwait and again in Germany, where they picked up their walking wounded. Captain George kept up the conversation and encouraged the flow of wine and women. As the junior officer flirted with flight attendants and Navy nurses alike, Lucky's thoughts were already a million miles closer to home.

"Making up for lost time, I see," said a Navy lieutenant-nurse from across the aisle. The lieutenant wasn't speaking to Lucky, but the flight attendant propped on his aisle seat armrest remembered her duties and excused herself.

"That depends," answered Captain George, the man on Lucky's right she was speaking to.

After a few minutes of bickering between the captain and the lieutenant, Lucky realized exactly what that depended on. Captain George, or George of the Urban Jungle as they called him in combat, had met his match. Navy lieutenant and Marine Corps captain were even the same pay grade. Lucky had a feeling this wasn't their first encounter. Or their last.

Standing, Lucky offered his seat to the redheaded lieutenant and slid into hers next to another nurse. The older woman, a Navy captain, was three pay grades above a Marine Corps captain and equal to a colonel. Which made her the senior female presence onboard and probably the head nurse for the entire medical unit that had deployed with them.

Lucky felt a little uncomfortable at first, but she smiled at him over her romance novel and continued reading while he broke out his laptop computer.

He had about a half a dozen e-mails from Cait. All asking for his flight information. Over the past three months they'd exchanged e-mails and Instant Messages. Not to mention, he'd spent a small fortune on phone calls, text messages and upgrades to the latest communications technology.

"You do realize you're obsessed with a woman you've never met." Damned if Bruce hadn't been right. There was a point when an obsession became unhealthy.

He'd backed off in recent weeks.

She hadn't taken the hint.

"Your wife?" the woman beside him asked as he toggled between a picture of a very pregnant Cait and a 3-D video ultrasound of "the peanut"—a nickname he'd given the baby after seeing that first ultrasound.

"No."

The captain nodded politely and went back to her reading.

Lucky continued to stare at that precious, pulsing video. His own heart beat double-time. Peanut was more defined these days. At least Lucky could tell the arms from the legs. But he still had to twist his head at odd angles to figure it all out in the greater scheme of things.

"Do you know if it's a boy or a girl?" the woman asked.

He shook his head.

"Would you like to?"

"Yeah," he admitted sheepishly. He had no business knowing anything he didn't hear firsthand from Cait.

The nurse pointed out the obvious and the not so obvious. "And there's his little smeckle."

Peanut had a penis.

Lucky felt overwhelming pride in his discovery.

"Who is she?" the woman asked, still curious about Cait's picture.

"My sister-in-law." He felt the edges of his smile fade. It was easy to develop feelings for someone who sent you e-mails, baked you cookies and wished you home safe. But Cait had never treated him like anything other than a big brother.

"Ah." Her expression softened. But she didn't make the usual small talk about his being the baby's uncle. Instead she looked at him with pity.

"I'm the donor," he said defensively. And while his admission didn't exactly fall under doctor–patient confidentiality, he felt his secret was safe.

"Oh," said his newfound confidant. And that *oh* was heavy with innuendo.

"My brother was killed in Iraq."

"So I've heard." It was as if she could also hear everything he'd left unsaid.

An awkward silence followed. "Brothers are a close DNA match," he blurted. "And a common sperm donor."

"Uh-huh." Her mouth curved into a soft smile as she went back to her book.

For the rest of the roughly thirty-six-hour flight, counting layovers, Lucky watched movies and napped. Fifteen minutes out of San Diego the pilot came over the speaker system. "It's been an honor and a privilege to serve you, Marine Expeditionary Unit One..." He named all the subordinate commands and detachments. "It's a sunny seventy-two degrees in San Diego on this first day of spring, March 2008. Let me be the first to welcome you home!"

The cheer that erupted was deafening.

The celebration lasted until they were on the ground. At the gate, nervous anticipation took over.

"Please remain seated," a flight attendant announced, "until our new fathers have deplaned."

Half the cabin was already standing and beginning to push forward. Lucky remained in his seat. The new fathers were handed individually wrapped yellow roses by another flight attendant at the cabin door.

"Go on," his seatmate urged. "You don't want to keep a pregnant girl waiting. She's probably been on her feet for hours."

He hesitated. Caitlin wasn't waiting for him. She'd wanted to meet him at the airport, but he'd told her not to bother. Meeting her for the first time was going to be awkward enough.

"Do I have to give you an order, Marine?"

"No, ma'am." He hopped to his feet and made his way forward. Mistaking him for one of the new fathers, a flight attendant forced a yellow rose on him. He was told to give it to the mother of his child. Technically, that would be Cait. But only technically.

The senior nurse waved him off the plane. "Good luck to you, Master Sergeant, and your little family."

CAITLIN WAITED IN THE BAGGAGE claim area around a carousel designated for the unit. It would have been hard to miss with all the Welcome Home signs. She should have thought to make a poster, but then that seemed too obvious, and he'd asked her not to come.

For the first time she realized he might have asked for a reason. He'd said he didn't want her to go to the trouble, that he'd stop by her apartment after he shook off the jet lag. After flying halfway around the world? She couldn't wait that long. He'd left Baghdad around one o'clock Sunday. It was now three o'clock Monday here in San Diego. Which meant it was one in the morning Tuesday in Baghdad. Thirty-six hours? He was going to be exhausted. Maybe it wasn't just an excuse.

But what if it was?

What if he had someone here waiting for him?

Curious, she looked around for any indication that she wasn't the only one. Judging by the number of women waving Welcome Home, Jack banners, Jack was one popular guy. Or there were a lot of guys named Jack with the unit.

Nothing for Luke or Lucky, though.

They'd been corresponding for three months now, but she didn't feel as if she knew him any better than she did during those first few phone calls. He rarely volunteered personal information. Bruce had described his brother as a lone wolf, a sniper who operated forward of his team. He'd tried to warn her not to get her hopes up. The fact that he wasn't here to welcome home his own brother was telling.

Caitlin took a hesitant step backward, trying to fade into the crowd. Which made her seem all the more conspicuous.

Several sideways glances were cast her way. A group of Jack fans whispered behind their poster-board signs.

There were a lot of new babies. Some only a month or two old. But no pregnant stragglers.

These men had been gone too long for that.

She stood out in her black dress with the tiny red rosebuds and her burgeoning belly. Tilting her chin, Caitlin held her ground. It wasn't as if she was wearing some scarlet letter. And she'd removed the price tag from the dress before putting it on.

As his sister-in-law she had just as much right to welcome him home as anyone else.

How had he explained *her* to the important people in his life? Had he explained their situation to anyone? Had she tied his hands when she'd asked him to keep it between them?

The first wave of men caused a stir of excitement. Before they were even in sight spontaneous applause erupted throughout the airport. The baggage carousel started to hum, then turn as the first bag dropped through the chute.

Men carrying yellow roses were swallowed up by big and small groups of families and friends. They grabbed their bags and were out the door for home as the second wave hit.

They all wore the same desert fatigue uniform. Would she recognize him from his pictures? Would he look more like her Luke in person? They shared so many common characteristics, but it was hard to tell from a few down-loaded snapshots. As the carousel started to fill, someone pulled off gear, calling out names and stacking the un-claimed bags to the side.

"Calhoun!" a Marine shouted as he lifted another bag.

Caitlin's pulse started to pound as a Marine picked up that seabag and hefted it over his shoulder. He carried a yellow rose in his free hand. And she knew the exact moment his green eyes spotted her. She hoped that quirky half smile meant he was happy to see her because in that instant he looked so much like her Luke she wanted to cry. It had been 274 days. If he had been her Luke she would have been wrapped up in his arms by now.

Calhoun closed the distance with long, measured strides.

Her own feet may as well have been tacked to the tile floor. His smile had been replaced by a look of resignation.

Luke Calhoun Jr. was older. More battle-hardened than her Luke had ever been. His brown hair, what there was of it, shades lighter. His tan darker. His green eyes sharp as they focused in on her.

She knew he'd be tall. She didn't know he'd look so solid, so imposing, with shoulders broad enough to carry a heavy seabag without hunching over. He stood out among a group of men all tan and fit and wearing the same uniform.

He couldn't be described as handsome, like Luke. Or Bruce. He was more rugged than that. More rough around the edges.

He stopped. Close enough that they should be touching.

He dropped his bag just as the baby kicked. She pressed both hands to her belly. "Peanut, meet your uncle Lucky."

"UNCLE LUCKY" FELT HIS CHEST tighten. "Peanut." He cleared his throat. His gaze shifted back up to meet hers. "Hi."

"Hi back," she said. "I know you said not to come…." She bit her full bottom lip.

"It's okay. I'm glad you're here."

Her eyes and her smile were sadder than in her wedding photos. But the real Cait, the pregnant Cait, was even more beautiful up close.

"Are you meeting someone?"

He followed her gaze to the yellow rose in his hand. "No, this is for you."

"Oh, thank you." She accepted it with a shrug, then leaned in for a sisterly hug. "Welcome home!"

The exchange was awkward at best. He didn't know what to do with his hands.

She smelled like apples and cinnamon. He had to tell himself not to bury his nose in her hair, or brush a kiss across her forehead. She felt good. Damn good.

And round. He loosened her hold around his neck.

"You're not a hugger," she said with a nervous laugh and pulled back.

"Not really," he admitted. He didn't like being the center of attention. "What do you say we get out of here?"

She stood staring over his shoulder. "What are those women doing, beating that Marine with their signs?"

He glanced back at the commotion. "That's just Jack."

"You know him? Aren't you going to help him?"

"Nope," he said, picking up his seabag and guiding her toward the exit. "Jack's going to have to get himself out of this one."

"But—"

"Trust me. He deserves it."

He dug his fatigue cap out of his back pocket and put it on as he stepped through the door. The air outside was warmer than the air-conditioned plane and airport. But even the seventy-degree temperature was fifty degrees cooler than the desert and gave him chills. His new environment would take some getting used to. Lucky scanned the parking garage out of habit.

They had a stretch to get to her car. He followed her toward a classic yellow Mustang. "That '64 1/2 your ride?" he asked.

"It was my mother's," she said. "After she died my father kept it locked away in our garage. He gave it to me as a graduation present. He spent a lot of time restoring it, but I think he found it cathartic."

"Sorry about your mother."

"It was a long time ago." She shrugged off his sympathy, but she couldn't hide the wistfulness in her voice. "My grandmother was the original owner," she said, bringing his attention back to the car. "Did you want to drive?" She dangled the keys.

"Better not," he said regretfully. "I'll ride shotgun." It had been a long time since he'd driven in traffic. Or anything smaller than an armored Humvee.

He felt like an idiot waiting for a woman to open his door and put the top down. He should have held on to the keys that long at least. It was the normal everyday things that would trip him up for a while. Until he became acclimated to normal again.

Cait climbed behind the wheel, her baby bump almost touching the steering column. She was—what?—six months pregnant now? He hoped she hadn't asked him to drive because it was uncomfortable for her. But her safety, even above her comfort, came first and that was the issue here. He tossed his seabag in back and got in the passenger side.

He studied her as she adjusted her seat belt across her lap. Things needed to be said. And he had no idea how to say them.

She put the key in the ignition but didn't start the car. "You're staring at me."

"Sorry," he apologized.

She tucked a strand of that honey-blond hair behind her ear. "Seat belt," she prompted, meeting his green eyes with her brown ones as he strapped in.

He didn't want to make her uncomfortable, so he fixed his gaze straight ahead while he continued to watch her out of the corner of his eye. Finally, she started the car and backed out. They passed several parked buses with Welcome Home banners. If Cait hadn't picked him up he'd be piling into one of those Greyhounds right now.

He reached over and tapped the horn.

Cait waved and honked a couple more times. The guys went wild with their catcalls and whistles. Lucky was glad they were headed out of earshot because the things being said were pretty crude.

He'd have to be careful not to drop the "F bomb" in every other sentence. Polite society did not talk or act the way he was used to talking and acting. He didn't want to give Cait the wrong impression.

By the time they hit the open highway, he'd given up on wearing his cap. With the wind blowing past his white walls— Marines didn't have enough hair for the wind to blow through it—he felt almost human again.

He reached for the volume on the radio at the same time as Cait. "Sorry," he apologized, pulling back.

"Don't be. I like this song." She turned the music way up.

"Rascal Flatts. 'Life Is a Highway.' Did you see the Disney movie *Cars?*"

He recognized the band, even recognized the movie. A lot of guys he knew had shipped the DVD home to their kids the Christmas before last. This past Christmas it had been *Meet the Robinsons*. Folks didn't realize the base exchange in Baghdad was as well-stocked as any Stateside Wal-Mart. "I guess there'll be a lot of Disney movies in your future."

"Yes, yes, there will." That admission was followed by a long silence. Not so much awkward as introspective.

Where did they start? "Do you know how to get to Camp Pendleton?"

"Wouldn't you rather come home with me?"

He was silent for another long minute, trying not to read too much into it.

"I didn't mean…" she backtracked.

"I know."

"I just meant—"

"I know."

"Just that if you had no place you'd rather be, you could stay with me for a while.…" She didn't stop trying to explain. He didn't mind; he kind of liked listening to her.

He stopped paying attention to what she was saying and started paying attention to the fact that she was nervous around him. Maybe even more than he was around her.

"Okay," he agreed.

"So there's no one?"

He went back to staring at her. This time because he couldn't quite figure out what she was talking about.

"Special, I mean. Wife? Ex-wife? Girlfriend?"

"Who'd have me?"

"I bet there are plenty of women—" She glanced at him, blushed, then looked into her rearview mirror as she put on her turn signal to take the upcoming exit. "Kids?"

He didn't know how to answer that. His gaze drifted to her lap and her hand went to her stomach.

"I didn't mean—"

"Then, no." This was new territory. Despite three months of e-mails, they hadn't found their common ground yet. Except for Luke and the baby they really didn't have anything in common.

She pulled off into a residential neighborhood and slowed to the posted speed. Trash cans lined the street on both sides. Lucky felt every muscle in his body tense. He reached for the steering wheel with his left hand.

"What are you doing?"

"There's a trash can in the street up ahead."

"I see it. It's not really out in the street."

Just the same, he didn't ease up on the wheel until she gave the overturned can a wide berth. "Occupational hazard," he apologized.

She looked at him, perplexed. "I offered to let you drive." Cait put on her turn signal, turning right into the Terrace Gardens apartment complex. She parked under a carport in a numbered space near the courtyard stairs.

Lucky grabbed his bag from the back seat and helped her put up the ragtop. She stopped at a wall of mailboxes to pick up her mail, which, he was glad to see, wasn't overflowing with bills. She carried her rose with the mail.

As they passed the first door on the right, some lady with

her hair up in rollers came out and stood there with her hands on her hips.

With "...*sands through the hour glass*..." in the background, she stared after them as they climbed the steps. The woman mumbled something in Tagalog, a dialect he recognized from the Philippines. That didn't mean he understood a word she was saying.

"That's Mrs. Pèna, my landlady." Caitlin forced a smile and waved.

Lucky stopped on the first landing and turned to the woman. "I'm going to be staying here for a couple of days. If that's all right with you?"

"Hmm," the landlady huffed, going back inside.

"Don't think she likes me," he said, catching up to Cait at the top of the third flight of stairs.

"She thinks I have too many military men around."

"Do you?" His gaze made that imperceptible slide down her body, then back up again. He didn't like the idea of her with too many men.

Key in lock, Cait regarded him for a full minute before she swung the door wide to let him in. "Not that it's any of your business."

"Sorry." He was doing a lot of apologizing for stepping out of bounds. Lucky stopped in the doorway. So close they were almost touching.

He brushed by, trying not to touch her. He could see why complete strangers felt compelled to touch pregnant women. But while he was little more than a stranger to Cait, his intentions weren't that pure.

"You don't have to keep apologizing," she said.

His gaze lingered a little too long on her lips.

He had no right to touch her, no right to taste her. No right to the kind of welcome-home most guys looked forward to. "Yeah, I do."

He stepped inside, and she closed the door behind them.

"You're welcome to stay as long as you'd like," she said without hesitation.

"I won't hold you to that." He set his seabag down next to the door. "I don't plan on sticking around California long." Just long enough to see for himself that she was going to be all right.

"Oh?" There was disappointment in her tone. "Are you taking leave to go somewhere?" She gestured toward the furniture in her living room, inviting him to sit. Simple. Tasteful. A couch and a chair. A small entertainment center. He remained standing, hat in hand.

She sat on the cushioned arm of the couch. "Are you on leave right now?"

"Liberty. It's downtime that isn't charged against leave. My hitch was up a couple months ago, extended because of the war."

"You're leaving the Marine Corps?"

"All that's left is the paperwork. Then I'm a free man." In more ways than one.

"When?"

"A couple of days. Two."

"Oh!" She seemed to be having a hard time wrapping her head around the idea. "That's a good thing. A really good thing. No more fighting," she said in an overly bright voice. "What are you going to do with all that freedom?"

"Ride with the big boys." He did a little throttle action with his hand. "Just me and Fat Bob taking the long road to Sturgis this summer."

"Fat Bob is a friend of yours?"

"Fat Bob is a motorcycle. A Harley-Davidson. I can't believe Luke didn't educate you," he said.

"Luke didn't ride a motorcycle."

"I guarantee you he knew how to ride. Competition level motocross. Amateur circuit. The best bikes Big Luke's money could buy. From the time he was knee-high."

He clenched his jaw against the bitter taste of that memory. He shouldn't have brought it up.

"Thank you." She surprised him with a watery smile. "Luke told me he broke his collarbone going over the handlebars of his bike. I thought he meant bicycle."

"Nope, he was a dirt rider."

"Dirt rider, huh?" She had a look of longing on her face he couldn't even begin to figure out. "Maybe if we'd had more time there wouldn't be all these blank spots…. I'm sorry," she said, pushing up from the chair. "I'm not being a very good hostess. What's the first thing you do when you get home from deployment?"

After a ten-month deployment? Aside from hunting down a good meal and a willing woman? "Shower off the road dirt. And sleep for about twenty-four hours straight."

"The bathroom is through the bedroom." She led the way. He picked up his bag and followed. "I'll get you some fresh towels," she said, already digging around in the linen closet in the bathroom. "Do you want to get something to eat after your shower?" she called.

"Sure."

Unlike the rest of the apartment, her bedroom was messy and overcrowded. For starters, the unmade four-poster bed was too big for the room. There was a walk-in closet and two dressers with clothes spilling out of every door and drawer.

"What's with all the wedding presents?" They were still wrapped, in wedding paper that showed wear and tear, and scattered around the room. The question was meant to be rhetorical. He didn't realize she was standing in the doorway between the bathroom and the bedroom, hugging a folded towel and watching him.

"They came after Luke left. I was waiting for him to get back to open them."

She laid the towel on the bed and he grunted something sympathetic. She gave him a weak smile before closing the bedroom door behind her.

Setting his gear down next to the bed, Lucky caught a glimpse of the historic Point Loma lighthouse through the French doors to her balcony. The lighthouse in Cabrillo National Park overlooked Fort Rosecrans Military Reservation. Navy SEALs liked to be buried there because of its view of the bay and the Naval Special Warfare Command.

If dead men could roll over in their graves, Luke was rolling over in his right now as Lucky unbuttoned his shirt in the widow-bride's bedroom. "I hope you knew what a lucky bastard you were."

Caitlin may have picked the apartment for the view.

But not for the ocean view.

"HE SAYS HE'S LEAVING IN two days!" She snipped off the end of the rose and put it in a bud vase. Yellow was the color of waiting. Very appropriate for a pregnant woman. "Can't you change his mind?"

Caitlin was still on the phone with Bruce when Calhoun stepped out of her bedroom. He'd changed into a clean desert-drab T-shirt and cammies. She hadn't waited three months to meet him just so he could leave again in two days.

"He has a mind of his own, Cait."

"Call me later," she pleaded in a hushed tone. "That was Bruce," she explained, hanging up. "I asked him to call back later. Do you want to order in? Pizza okay?" She was already punching in Pizza Hut on her speed dial.

"Pizza's fine." Calhoun frowned at the cell phone in his hand. "Do you have somewhere I could plug this in?"

She pointed to her charger on the counter next to the cookie jar. "There's an adaptor in the junk drawer below if you need it. What do you want on your pizza?" *Pizza Hut,* she mouthed when someone came on the line to take her order. "Large. Half pineapple and ham. And half…"

"Meat lover's," he said.

"Meat lover's," she repeated into the phone.

She ended the call and turned to find Calhoun with his hand in the cookie jar. "Ahem." She cleared her throat.

"You don't know how hard I had to fight to keep these all to myself." He shoved half a chocolate-chip cookie into his mouth. "Bruce say he'd been trying to reach me?" he asked, chewing.

"He didn't say. Would you like a glass of milk?" she asked, happy to hear her cookies were appreciated. Still chewing, he nodded. "Excuse me." She indicated the cupboard behind him. He ducked out of her way as she reached in for two tumblers. Opening the fridge, she poured the two glasses full of milk and handed one to him.

"Thanks," he said.

"Cheers!" They bumped glasses.

He smelled like a new bar of Irish Spring, his damp hair spiky. She bet all he had to do was towel it dry, rake some gel through it and he was good to go. She wondered if it was as soft to the touch as it looked.

Or if it was prickly from the gel.

Her baby could have hair that exact shade of light brown with that high hairline. Or those same penetrating green eyes that were studying her now.

"Did Bruce say when he'd call back?" He leaned back against the counter as he polished off another cookie.

"No."

He appeared casual, relaxed. But something about the way he moved told her he was more controlled than relaxed. There was a hint of ink above his collar and below his sleeve.

Biker tattoos?

Her Luke didn't have any tattoos. She knew that much. If Luke was a dirt biker what was Calhoun?

A street biker? One of those Hell's Angels? Was he leaving the military to join a biker gang?

Her kitchen had never felt so small.

Nonsense. In all the time they'd been exchanging e-mails and phone calls he'd never said or done anything to make her feel uncomfortable. So why was she feeling that way now?

"I bet it's been a while since you've had pizza," she said, trying to take the edge off.

"Camp Victory has its own Pizza Hut and just about every other fast food you can name."

"No way. Subway?"

He nodded. After a moment of silence, he added, "Mind if I watch the game until the pizza gets here?"

Okay, so he wasn't a hugger or a talker.

The game was college basketball. Something called March Madness. Excusing herself, Cait went into her bedroom to change into black capris and a white-on-black, butterfly-print maternity top. When she came back out, he was flipping through the pages of a book on her coffee table.

Her father's Christmas present had been the same thing he got her every year. A gift certificate to Amazon.com. She'd picked up a couple of books on genetics and one on genealogy.

"Pretty heavy reading," he commented.

She sat opposite him on the heavy trunk table that served as a coffee table and slid a coaster under his glass of milk. To his credit he muted the sound on March Madness and gave her his complete attention.

"I was just trying to make sense of it all. For me it's not about that anymore, it's about family. Because of you, a part of Luke will go on."

Caitlin fidgeted with the white bow under her bustline. "I'm having a boy." Preparing herself with a deep breath, she smoothed her top over her baby bulge. "I'd like to name him Luke Lane Calhoun Jr. in honor of Luke. I just wasn't sure how you'd feel about that. With our special circumstances, I mean."

Biting her lip, she waited for his reaction.

He didn't react.

"It's not my decision," he said evenly.

CHAPTER FIVE

"THEN YOU'RE OKAY WITH IT?" she asked.

"Why wouldn't I be? I just supplied half the genetic code, right—the Calhoun DNA."

"You're more than that."

Yeah, family. Uncle Lucky. He was trying to come to terms with his role in all of this. Even though giving up his own kid went against everything he believed. It made him no better than Big Luke.

Okay, so her choice of names bothered him a little. A lot.

The doorbell rang.

"Saved by a pizza," she said blithely.

"Got it," he said, pushing to his feet. After he paid the delivery driver, he followed her into the kitchen.

She held out a twenty-dollar bill. "This is my treat."

"Don't worry about it." He set the pizza box down on the breakfast counter. She laid the twenty down on top of it, making it clear she didn't want anything from him. Except his Calhoun DNA.

"Are we going to go a round about money again?" he asked. Their bout had started when he'd begun paying her rent.

"I can take care of myself, Calhoun."

He shrugged. "I just paid for a pizza."

"That's not how this works."

Lucky knew when a man was itching to pick a fight. And he knew when a woman was itching to pick a fight with a man. He preferred a good barroom brawl.

This wasn't about a damn pizza. This was about boundaries.

He sat down on a stool, which brought them eye level. "So how does this work?"

She looked away first.

"You know," she said, getting the pizza cutter out of the drawer, "when your husband dies they don't just cut you a check. I went from being part of a two-income couple to a no-income widow in a heartbeat."

She reached for the pizza box. The twenty-dollar bill dropped to the counter. "We knew each other all of three weeks before we were married. Money wasn't exactly the topic of conversation. We just spent it like we had it." She opened the box and slashed through the pizza slices. "The honeymoon, the move…furniture for the house on officers' row." She stopped cutting to look him in the eye. "Half our married life was spent apart. But those forty-five days together were the happiest of my life. Those memories are priceless to me now."

She ended on a quieter note. "I've taken fiscal responsibility. Everything is under control. Will you please let me pay for the pizza?"

Lucky picked up the twenty. "I'll add it to Peanut's scholarship fund."

Cait sighed heavily as she reached for the paper plates to divvy up the pizza. "That's what you did with the rent money I paid back? Has anyone ever mentioned you have a real machismo thing going on when it comes to money?"

She pulled out the other stool and sat down.

"If you're not going to let me pay child support, then it's going to the kid's college education. Besides, I'll get every dime back when I take CryoBank to court." He was only half joking.

"I can't believe you're still going through with that."

"Why wouldn't I?"

"Why would you?" She stopped midbite. "They've offered to settle."

"Until they can tell me what happened to my—" he cleared his throat "—then I'm going through with the lawsuit."

He took a bite out of his meat-lovers' pizza. They couldn't even agree on simple pizza toppings—how were they ever going to agree on anything as complicated as a wrongful paternity suit?

He really wished she'd been more aggressive with Cryo-Bank from the start. Or that he'd been there to be her aggressor. She really didn't seem to have it in her nature.

"I can tell you what happened to your semen. They washed it and inserted it with a catheter through the cervix and into the uterus. The sperm passed into the fallopian tubes, where fertilization took place."

He'd stopped chewing. "More information than I needed to know, Cait."

"What? You asked. The procedure is called intrauterine insemination, IUI. You can take the prescribed drug clomiphene citrate or a follicle-stimulating hormone, FSH, to increase the chances of getting pregnant. Well, *you* can't. But I took an FSH because Luke only had the two samples in storage."

"I meant, I wanted to know why my specimen wasn't destroyed when I'd ordered it to be."

She scrunched her brow. "Why would you put your sperm in storage, then order it destroyed?"

His cell phone rang.

"Excuse me." Lucky got up to answer it.

"Why is Cait calling me upset?" Bruce demanded from the other end of the line.

"*Cait,* now, is it?" he asked his brother. It was the same question his brother had once asked him. She heard her name and turned to listen openly. "I don't know. Why is Cait calling you all upset?" He directed the question at Cait.

She looked embarrassed.

Bruce sounded annoyed. "Are you repeating everything because she's listening?"

"Yup."

His brother cursed under his breath. "Put Cait on."

Lucky handed over his cell phone.

"Hi," she said into it. "No, we're good." She passed the phone back. "He wants to talk to you again."

"So, you're at Cait's…"

"She picked me up at the airport."

"How was the flight?" Bruce asked.

"Long."

"Did you want to get together tomorrow and do something, just the two of us? And maybe we should take Cait out to dinner this weekend."

"I won't be here this weekend."

"That figures. I don't know why, but she's been waiting all these months to meet you. Could you just think about sticking around before pulling your hi/goodbye routine?"

This time Lucky had a very good reason for wanting to get the hell out of Dodge. "I'll catch up with you tomorrow." He hung up.

"So, back to CryoBank…" Caitlin said as soon as Calhoun came back to sit down.

"Cait, it's my first night back. Enough CryoBank. Why don't we eat and go walk off dinner?"

After they'd finished, Cait grabbed a black bolero sweater and they walked those few blocks to the beach. He'd buttoned into a camouflage shirt over his T-shirt, with his sleeves rolled up. And he put on his cap as soon as they stepped outside.

He wore combat boots while she'd taken off her flip-flops as soon as they reached the sand. "I cut through this way all the time," she said when he would have bypassed the private access. He took her arm and helped her over a low chain between posts that lined the sidewalk, more decorative than an actual deterrent.

They walked along the water line, where the sand was packed firm by the tide and the water was cool on her bare feet. The sound of the waves lulled them into an easy rhythm as the sun sank low in the sky. It was a while before either of them spoke.

"So what have I done to upset you?" He strolled with his hands behind his back, letting her smaller steps set the pace.

Busted. But then she knew that already.

"It's not anything you've done. I just thought with you back from Iraq, we'd—" she gestured toward her baby "—have some time to get to know you."

"Bruce thinks the three of us should go out to dinner this weekend. How about I stick around until then?"

Five days.

"I'd like that, but I meant *real* time, Calhoun. Most women know more about their anonymous donors than I know about my own brother-in-law."

He scanned the distance. "The only thing you need to know about me, Cait, is that I'm remorseless."

Merciless. Persistent. Relentless.

"*Remorseless.*" She rolled the word, and all that it implied, around on her tongue. The opposite was remorse, a sense of guilt for past wrongs.

"It's the one trait required to be a sniper."

She pictured him on a rooftop in the desert, sighting down the barrel of his weapon and pulling the trigger. She shivered.

"No regrets? Ever?"

"Just one."

He met her eyes. But she still couldn't fathom what that one regret was. "You're not going to tell me, are you?"

"No." He shook his head.

"Does it involve shooting someone?"

He offered a wry smile at her attempt to play Twenty Questions. "No, I only take out enemy targets."

Their game went no further than the first question.

"What is it you're going to do when you're no longer a Marine? Aside from that motorcycle rally in Sturgis. Which, by the way, Bruce informed me is only one week every year in *August*."

"For starters, I'm not going to think about the future."

She folded her arms above her stomach, under her bustline, and looked at the serious set to his mouth. "You have to think about it. You have to have some kind of plan for your future."

"My plan is to take a year off."

"Then there's really no reason why you couldn't stay longer than five days," she urged, hopeful.

"There are a lot of reasons, Cait."

This time when he looked at her, he looked her up and down with that telltale pause in the middle. She'd bet money all those "reasons" had to do with her and CryoBank. She gave herself and Peanut a little hug. Peanut, who had been content to sleep through their walk, kicked back.

"Would you like to feel the baby move?" she asked the stranger beside her. Her brother-in-law. Her donor.

Peanut's *father...*

"Cait." He stopped walking to face her. "Are you cold?" he asked as she stood hugging herself in those last few rays of light.

He was already unbuttoning his shirt by the time she answered. "A bit."

She couldn't meet those sharpshooter eyes as he wrapped her in camouflage, so she stared at the dog tags dangling against his T-shirt.

"Cait," he started again and she felt compelled to look him in the eye because he'd removed his cap. "I can't be this baby's uncle. Not the kind of uncle you want me to be, anyway. Don't expect more from me than to breeze in and out again with presents on birthdays and at Christmases."

"What happened to being an involved uncle?"

A very involved uncle were his exact words that first phone call.

"It's not in anyone's best interest for me to become too involved in this pregnancy. Or with this baby," he said.

"I see." She didn't know what else to say. Didn't even

know what she wanted. Only that she'd set out to prove she could do this alone. That she didn't need him. She'd been the one to push for boundaries.

She took a hesitant step back in the direction they'd come and he followed. No longer able to meet his gaze, she kept her eyes averted to the sand, retracing their footprints until the rising tide erased their tracks.

Careful what you wish for.

"YOU SURE I CAN'T TALK YOU INTO the bedroom?" Lucky groaned, remembering their earlier conversation.

Okay, that hadn't come out exactly as he'd intended. Cait had insisted he take the bed while she slept on the couch. The only reason he'd agreed was because she'd convinced him she couldn't sleep in her bed.

He punched the pillow a couple more times, trying to get comfortable. He hadn't slept in a bed in forever. The mattress was too soft. The pillow was too soft.

And he was too damn hard.

He'd heard voices coming from the living room earlier. By the time he'd realized it was the television, she'd muted the sound. It was now well after 0200 hours, and from what he could see through the partially cracked door, light and shadow still played across the living room walls.

He kicked aside the girlie covers. The color pink made him itch worse than a government-issued wool blanket. He may as well watch TV if he wasn't going to be sleeping. Or doing something that might put him to sleep.

If Cait hadn't shanghaied him at the airport he'd be with

an old girlfriend right about now. One who didn't care about commitments.

Only those were getting fewer, and harder to come by.

Every time he came back from deployment it seemed like another old flame had gotten married while he was gone.

He sat on the edge of the bed.

Pitching a tent in his boxers wasn't exactly perfect houseguest behavior. But one flash of light from the lighthouse in the distance across all those unopened wedding gifts solved that problem.

Cait wanted more from him than he could give.

He just couldn't give her any more of himself than he already had. She was trying to create a family unit of extended relatives for Peanut. And he didn't want any part of that. Peanut would grow up calling him Uncle Lucky.

It wasn't just that she wanted to name the baby after Luke. Or that Big Luke would treat this kid as Luke's—the kid was probably better off that way. Cait was young, not to mention beautiful. And someday soon her heart would be whole again. When that day came she'd find some guy who'd be a husband to her and a father to Peanut.

Lucky didn't want to be standing on the sidelines while his son called some other man Dad. So, while he owed it to Luke to look after the widow his brother had left behind, he owed it to himself to do it from a distance.

The thing about living a life of no regrets, you had to keep moving. Or all those regrets started to catch up with you.

Lucky scrubbed a hand over his tired face and pushed up from the bed. He pulled on his running shorts and padded barefoot to the living room. Cait was sound asleep.

Curled up on her side, with her leg flung over the covers, she looked tempting.

Over his shoulder, Luke sliced through their wedding cake with his sword. *Show-off.*

Lucky picked up the remote from the coffee table and clicked off the DVD player. Then he picked up Cait and carried her to the bedroom.

She settled against his tattooed right side with a sigh, looking all the more innocent against the tribal art.

Her breath on his neck. Cinnamon.

The smell of her hair. Apples.

The softness of her skin.

The rightness of their child against his heart.

Carrying her tensed his muscles in a good way. The hard part was letting her go as he laid her gently on her bed. On that too-soft pillow. And that too-soft mattress.

His body ached to bury himself in all that softness. To experience the act of creation with the mother of his child the way it was meant to be between a man and a woman.

Lucky took control of his baser instincts and pulled the hem of her ratty old T-shirt down over her panties to cover her.

One of Luke's T-shirts?

He reached across her body for the sheet, wishing he'd felt the baby move when she'd given him the chance. A chance like that wasn't likely to come his way again. Not after he'd disappointed her.

Cait rolled from her side to her back and opened her eyes. "Luke?"

"Just settling the argument of who's sleeping where tonight."

"Oh," she said on a dreamy sigh and fell back asleep.

CAITLIN HAD HAD THE DREAM WHERE Luke was standing over her bed again. She'd slept better than she had since her first trimester, but how she'd wound up in her bed she could only imagine.

"Oh," she groaned into her pillow as the reality sank in. Could she have embarrassed herself any more than if she'd drooled on him? Had she actually snuggled against her brother-in-law's bare chest?

What business did he have carrying her, anyway? Just because he was strong enough to pick her up didn't mean he could take control in her home and change their sleeping arrangements.

By the time she got out of bed she was good and mad. By the time she got to the living room she realized he was good and gone.

The pillow and blanket were neatly folded on one end of the couch. His seabag wasn't by her bed or next to the door, the last two places she remembered seeing it. She should feel relieved. But she didn't.

When she stepped into her kitchen, she noticed he'd moved the bud vase with the yellow rose to the center of her breakfast bar, next to a bakery bag. She calmed down some. The sight of a bagel and cream cheese could do that to a pregnant gal.

He'd stuck a Post-it note to the bag. *Eat Me*.

On a glass of milk in her fridge, another Post-it note read *Drink Me*. She felt like a regular Alice In Wonderland.

Sitting at the breakfast counter with her bagel and cream cheese and her glass of milk, she opened her laptop to read her e-mail and grabbed the stack of unopened snail mail from yesterday.

She managed all her money online these days. She paid a couple of bills that were due while she opened her mail, but most of it was junk, which went straight to the recycle bin. On the bottom of the stack was a padded manila envelope with a return address of Colorado. She didn't recognize it as Nora Jean's or Dottie's addresses, and the handwriting was different.

She opened it and a key fell out. She dug out the enclosed letter and photo of a small cottage house. The letter, a note really, was from Big Luke.

> What did you want to do with the house? It's been on the market for six months now. Congratulations on the pregnancy, by the way. I hope to see you and my grandbaby soon.
> Big Luke

Big Luke had given them the house as a belated wedding present, and after Luke died had offered to put it on the market for her. She hadn't really thought about it since then.

The street address was on the back of the photo. She'd never been to Colorado and didn't even know where Englewood was on a map. She went to MapQuest and found out it was a small city in the shadow of Denver.

"Hmm." She put everything back in the envelope, feeling a little guilty. She'd never thought to tell Big Luke about the pregnancy. They hadn't been in touch since the flowers he'd sent following Luke's funeral and her thank-you note.

Obviously, he'd found out.

Not that it was a big secret or anything. The only family

she'd told was her mother-in-law. And her father, who was slowly coming around. He was just worried about her being out here all by herself.

The closer she got to her due date in June the more she worried about that, too. She gave Peanut a pat. "Not to worry. Mrs. Pèna can drive us to the hospital."

As long as the baby didn't decide to come between eleven in the morning and three in the afternoon they'd be fine. She broke off a piece of bagel and stuffed it in her mouth. Who would drive her to the hospital?

Bruce wasn't driving yet.

Pam's husband was getting his own command and they'd be transferring soon. Jill's husband retired last month, and they'd moved back to the Midwest somewhere. Marilyn had fallen out of touch after getting the number to Cait's fertility specialist and one unsuccessful attempt to get pregnant.

"Grandma Nora was planning on flying out after you were born. Maybe we could get her to come early."

She thought of one other person. Would he stay if she asked? She played with the sticky backs of the Eat Me/Drink Me notes. He wouldn't want to. But he would. Except she wasn't going to ask.

Not after their walk on the beach last night. She'd rather deliver in the back of a taxi.

Her cell phone vibrated across the counter and she leaned over to get it. A text message from Calhoun read Call me, lunch my treat!

Have to work, she texted Calhoun back.

She got up to throw away her trash and rinse her glass in the sink. She was putting it in the dishwasher when she noticed one last Post-it note attached to the cover of her gene-alogy book, which he'd moved to her kitchen counter so she'd find it.

It said *Read Me.* She took the book with her and sat back down at the bar. She opened it to the papers she'd kept tucked inside and her eyes started to get watery.

She'd printed out a sample donor profile form she'd found online at CryoBank's Web site.

He'd filled out his medical history. Taken the personality test. Included a photocopy—where did he get a photocopy?—of his military ID and a very old, very worn wallet-size studio photo of two healthy, happy little boys.

The bigger brother was holding on to the younger one to keep him from crawling off. She turned it over and read the back. The faded handwriting read *Bruce, age 1. Luke, age 5.*

Her heart skipped a beat. The photo must have been taken before he'd gotten his nickname.

Her baby was the next-generation Calhoun. And he might even look like one of those young boys.

She felt the tug at her heartstrings and punched in #1 on her speed dial. Where was the harm in taking the chance to get to know him in the short time she had left? "I get an hour for lunch," she said when he picked up.

LUCKY ENTERED THE WALGREENS where Cait worked just before her lunch hour. She wasn't working one of the open cash registers up front. He'd been running official errands all morning as part of his outprocessing so he was once again wearing his uniform.

"Caitlin Calhoun?" he asked a stock boy in a blue vest. The

young man plucked an iPod earbud from his ear and pointed toward the back. Lucky hoped to hell they didn't have her working in the stockroom in her condition. He hurried to the back of the store, where he stopped another guy with a mop bucket coming through the swinging double doors. "I'm looking for Cait—"

"So you're the hero's brother," said a tech from behind the pharmacy desk. "I'm Roger, by the by. Caitlin's told me *all* about you."

Her hero's brother? What did that make him, the antihero?

"Do you know where I can find her?" he asked with a hint of the irritation he felt.

"Caits, your brother-in-law is here!" Roger called.

But all he'd had to do was look up. Cait was in the pharmacy wearing blue scrubs and a white lab coat. She looked away from a computer screen. "Hi." She offered him a tentative smile. "I'll just be a minute."

He watched her as she finished inputting something and then turned to hang up her lab coat and pick up her purse.

"You never mentioned you were a pharmacist."

"I've mentioned temping here on and off several times since Christmas. Walgreens is a pharmacy. Did you think I was just another dumb blonde?" she teased.

Well, he wouldn't make that mistake again. Not that he'd ever thought she was dumb. But he'd had a lot of preconceived notions about her. She was better educated and better able to take care of herself than he'd thought.

He could leave with a clear conscience after this weekend. Hell, he hadn't even graduated high school. He was just a guy with a GED who'd become a Marine.

She didn't need him.

"Where would you like to go eat?" he asked.

"There's a little sandwich shop around the corner. It shouldn't be too busy this early."

They headed toward the door.

Outside, she spotted a motorcycle parked at the curb.

"Is that a Fat Bob?"

"No, that's a custom job. Still needs a lot of work."

"You mean it's yours?" She stopped to admire it.

"Yeah." Embarrassed by the attention his bike was getting, he kept them headed in the direction of lunch. He'd been working on motorcycles for as long as he could remember.

It was no big deal to scavenge old parts so he could keep himself in wheels. He had a few designs of his own he'd like to work on someday. Maybe someday was just around the next corner.

Nothing commercial.

Something small. In a seedy back alley where only the most unpretentious of riders would venture. He'd build his business by reputation and word of mouth, one motorcycle at a time.

"What are you going to name it? When you're done, I mean. Or does it already have a name?"

"I'm not going to name it."

"You have to," she insisted. "You're the creator. You get to call it anything."

Did she even hear the irony in that statement? Well, he knew what he wouldn't be calling it.

"I'm starving," he said, changing the subject.

"Oh, I wanted to ask you something." She dug an envelope out of her purse as they approached the bistro.

"What do you know about this house Big Luke gave to Luke and I as a wedding present?"

Just that he'd spent his childhood there.

He couldn't believe Big Luke had held on to it all these years. His last memory of the place was being in the car with his mother, and his parents driving off in different directions. "Not much of a house. You thinking of selling it? Or renting out the place?"

"I don't know. It's been on the market for a while now. What do you think?"

CAITLIN DAYDREAMED HER WAY through the afternoon lull in the pharmacy. Lunch had been nice. Calhoun thought she should contact a rental agency to rent out the cottage until she found a buyer. Because she was having second thoughts about selling.

Just before her shift ended, Marilyn came in to fill a prescription for prenatal vitamins and shared her good news. "Thank you so much for recommending the FSH." Her friend was glowing.

"I should have thought to tell you sooner," Caitlin said, truly happy for the other woman.

They exchanged a few pleasantries and a hug.

Cait's smile faded as her friend left, wondering if she'd ever been that happy about her own pregnancy. She envied Marilyn that.

The thought of FSH reminded her of the conversation she'd had with Calhoun. She'd thought he wanted to know about the IUI procedure, when what he'd really wanted to know was why his specimen hadn't been destroyed.

At the time she was curious about his choice. But now that she thought about it she was more than curious about whose specimen had actually been destroyed.

Her heart started to pound.

Ten minutes later she was hanging up her lab coat.

Within thirty minutes she found herself outside the doors of CryoBank.

Caitlin walked in and up to the counter. "Hi, I need some information regarding my husband's specimen."

They had all the information on file to give her access to Luke's account. She just needed to show her ID. The young female in green scrubs spent several minutes trying to pull up the data on the computer. Every second that ticked by felt like an eternity.

"According to our records, Mrs. Calhoun, your husband's two sperm samples were destroyed six months ago at his request."

"My husband *died* nine months ago." Cait gripped the counter to hold herself upright. She'd be damned if they were going to shove another tuna fish–smelling sack in her face. "I want to speak with Jenny," she demanded.

"Jenny's gone," the tech said. "I think she was fired."

"No, her husband transferred," said a black male technician also wearing green scrubs. "May I help you?"

"There must be some mistake. Could you look under Luke Calhoun Jr.? CyroBank sent my doctor the wrong—"

"I'm afraid you're not authorized access to any of our other client accounts, Mrs. Calhoun."

Caitlin punched #1 on her speed dial. "I need you now, Calhoun!"

LUCKY DIDN'T WASTE ANY TIME heading over to CryoBank. He'd left his brother in a sports bar with a half-assed explanation as to why he wasn't sticking around for happy hour and hot wings.

The hours of operation on the door indicated CryoBank was closed for the day. But it was unlocked, and Cait ran straight up to him when he walked in. "They destroyed Luke's sperm. Except I don't know if it's Luke's sperm or if it's your sperm because they won't confirm anything without your consent."

He eyeballed the bored rent-a-cop in the corner.

A well-heeled woman and two young technicians looked at him expectantly. He nodded his consent and walked over to the woman who appeared to be in charge of this operation.

Carol Livingston introduced herself as the director, then went behind the counter. She brought up something on the computer, then spun the monitor around so Cait could see it for herself.

Over her shoulder he read the exact date and time his first sample had been sent to Cait's doctor. There was a follow-up log note to indicate Success. And the storage location of his remaining sample.

"But how do you know this is right?" Cait demanded, still unwilling to accept it.

"Because the samples are correctly identified," said the director. "The error was in which one was destroyed and which one was delivered to the fertility clinic. It appears the orders came in on the same day." She explained their complicated color-coded system to prevent such errors. Yet the system had failed to catch this one human error.

"I assure you," she continued, "the person responsible has

been fired. I think I can give you conclusive evidence, Caitlin. If that will put this subject to rest."

Carol Livingston asked Lucky to confirm his donor number, which she verified on screen. "If you wouldn't mind going over to the handprint scanner and entering your donor number."

Lucky did as he was asked and placed his palm on the hand key, then punched in his donor number. The machine took only a second to positively ID him, then print out his donor labels. The information matched that on the computer screen.

Then the director asked him to enter Luke's donor number. Once again he placed his palm on the hand key and punched in the numbers she'd rattled off. This time the handprint scanner took longer.

He didn't even realize he'd been holding his breath until the match came back Negative.

All the fight went out of Cait, replaced by a look of defeat. Four tours in Iraq and he felt helpless to defend her. "This isn't over," he threatened the director. "Think jury trial."

"Mrs. Calhoun signed away her right to sue," the director said evenly.

"But I didn't." Lucky reached into the breast pocket of his cammies. "I've been waiting three months to do this."

He took out the folded and worn check with CryoBank's initial offer to him of thirty-five hundred dollars and ripped it up, letting the pieces fall around the scanner. Cait had received ten times that. She should have received ten times more. And he was going to get it for her. Maybe CryoBank had offered him so little because they didn't consider him a victim. Well, he wasn't a victim. He was a Marine. And what CryoBank should have considered was that he'd fight for what was right.

"By the way, I want that specimen destroyed," he ordered, pointing to the machine.

"I'm afraid we can't destroy your semen, Sergeant," Carol Livingston said. "As long as your lawsuit is pending, it's evidence."

He narrowed his eyes. "It's Master Sergeant."

Lucky turned to leave, but Cait was already out the door.

CAITLIN WALKED OVER TO THE bus-stop bench at the curb and sat before her legs gave out. Calhoun was only seconds behind her. He sat on the opposite end.

Neither of them said anything.

She stared off into space.

He raked his hands through that stubble on his head, then leaned forward with his head bowed, elbows resting on his knees.

"Cait—"

"There's nothing you can say to make this better." She'd have felt as empty as when she'd lost Luke, but the baby was kicking, reminding her she wasn't alone this time. "All I have left of him is through you, Calhoun. I don't want you to destroy your specimen." She held her stomach with both arms.

"Excuse me for being crude, but there's more where that came from. I'm not going to leave it with CryoBank."

"I want custody," she said.

"Oh, that's a good one, Cait. You already have custody of my unborn child. You want custody of my sperm, too?" He got up from the bench, turned as if to walk away. Then turned back. "Why?" he demanded. "Because there's some ten percent probability my baby will have Luke's eyes?"

She swallowed the lump in her throat. "Luke had eyes the color of emeralds. And he never narrowed them on me with accusation like you're doing now."

"I don't have to read a book on DNA," he said, "or graduate from high school to know that baby you're carrying is fifty-fifty me and you. Yet I have no rights under the law." He rubbed the back of his tanned neck. "You want to know what the JAG officer said to me? Forget about it. Cash the check."

After consulting with the Judge Advocate General's office on her own, Caitlin knew Calhoun's rights as a donor were limited by her choices as a mother. "So why didn't you?"

The sound of air brakes interrupted their conversation. A bus pulled up to the stop, and they waited for the passengers to disperse.

She had thought it would be Luke's name on her baby's birth certificate. He'd been her husband and the intended father. But it became complicated because of death benefits a child of Luke's would be entitled to. The simple solution would be to name the father "donor" or "artificial insemination." Calhoun would have no rights. But the lawyer had cautioned against it. Because her baby would have no father.

Her other option was to name her baby's biological father.

And leave herself wide open to his paternity challenge.

"Because I can't forget," he said, sliding in next to her once they were alone again. "I'm okay with being the donor, Cait. I'm not okay with being a factory outlet."

"I don't want this baby to grow up alone."

"Peanut's not growing up alone," he said with certainty. "Do you think Luke would want you to spend the rest of your life pining for him?"

She fumbled through her purse for her car keys and stood. He stood, too.

"I loved him."

"I don't doubt that, Cait."

"All I wanted was to have his baby."

"I know," he said. "Which is why I'm not going through this again. We're not talking about Luke's baby."

"I need to get home." She headed for her car.

"You should rethink your choice of baby names. Luke wouldn't want this baby named after him," he called.

She turned and walked right up to him. "Suddenly you're an expert on what Luke would want?" She shook her head and turned again to leave him standing there.

"I'm not sure you should be driving," he said, keeping pace with her.

"I'm fine."

"Just the same, I'll follow you home."

"Can I just ask you one thing?" She stopped to face him. "Why did you put your semen in storage in the first place? And what happened to make you change your mind?"

He didn't try to shy away from her direct line of questioning. "I wasn't sure I was coming back."

"But you did."

"But I did."

And that was the answer to both her questions.

CHAPTER SIX

AFTER THREE DAYS OF CAIT'S not returning his messages, Lucky called in reinforcements.

After a chat with Bruce, Cait agreed to go out to dinner and a movie with the two of them on Friday. So there they were, cooling their heels, both in civilian clothes, in her apartment.

"I don't have anything to wear," she said, studying their casual dress.

Lucky followed her into the bedroom, determined not to let her get away. "You have a whole closet full of clothes. There's gotta be something in here you can wear." He stared into her closet, wishing he knew what he was looking for.

"Nothing fits. I'm too fat."

"You're not fat."

"Don't you dare use one of those euphemisms like pleasantly plump."

"I don't even know what a euphemism is, but I'll be sure not to use one around you."

She pulled two more dresses out of her closet and tossed them on the growing discard pile on her bed. "I'm too pregnant," she whined.

"No one is too pregnant."

"Wasn't that the first thing you asked me? *How pregnant are you?* Well, the answer is *too pregnant!*"

Bruce leaned against the doorjamb. "Cait, are you sure you're not carrying twins?"

"See, see?" She poked Lucky's chest with a hanger to make her point. "Your brother thinks I'm fat!"

Lucky glowered over his shoulder at Bruce. "Not helping."

Bruce shrugged and limped away from the door.

"Everything I own is black!" she wailed.

"What's wrong with this one?" he asked, taking a dress down from the back of the closet door.

"It's black."

"You were wearing it when I got off the plane."

"I'd give you credit for that, Calhoun, but that was just four days ago."

"So you know it fits."

"You've already seen me in it. So has Bruce."

"I wouldn't mind seeing you in it again," he said.

Cait stopped her rant to confront him directly. "Why are you being so nice to me, Calhoun?"

"I never thought I was being all that mean to you before." Even though it had seemed as if they were at cross-purposes. He really did have her best interests at heart.

She had her hair pulled back into a ponytail today. No makeup. He didn't like the look of those purple smudges underneath her eyes. He'd bet she'd been up all night again. If he had to, he was coming back here tonight, invited or not, to put her to bed. Even if that meant camping out on her couch to keep her there.

"You're not mean. I'm being a bitch. And because I'm pregnant I blame it on hormones. Now get out so I can dress."

Finally.

"She coming?" Bruce asked when Lucky joined him in the kitchen.

"She's changing now," Lucky said. Bruce had a shot glass of tequila in front of him. "Where'd you get that?"

"I know where Cait keeps her liquor. For guests," he clarified. "Want one?"

Lucky shook his head. He might be designated driver tonight. Not that Cait would be drinking. Just that he might be driving.

"You a regular, then?" Lucky asked, dressed up in black slacks and an untucked, black-and-white shirt with three-quarter sleeves. Lucky thought of it as his bowling shirt, even though he didn't bowl.

"What are you asking me?" Bruce demanded.

"I thought you were avoiding her."

"I tried, but she wouldn't let me." Bruce was dressed down in a chambray shirt and jeans. He was off his crutches and had moved on to his training leg. An adjustable pole with a foot.

Lucky glanced down at his brother's empty left pant leg and looked away.

"It's okay, you can look." Bruce threw back the last of his drink and banged his glass down on the counter.

"So she knows all the details surrounding Luke's death?"

"I tried for months to avoid her, but she figured out I was there and confronted me. She had questions, and the Navy wasn't giving her answers. Or at least not to her satisfaction. She wanted to know if he had any last words."

"Did he?"

"Yeah—tell Lucky he's an asshole."

"Funny."

"No," Bruce said seriously. "He was just gone."

"What'd you tell her?"

"Tell Cait I love her."

"You idiot." Lucky smacked his brother upside the head. "How'd you explain taking so long to pass that along?"

"I was traumatized."

Lucky shook his head. "I don't know why you want to go back there. You don't have anything left to prove."

"Is that why you're getting out? Nothing left to prove?"

"Something like that."

"You're going to miss it, you know. You don't know how to be anything other than a Marine. You'll be like one of those ex-cons who gets himself thrown back in prison because he doesn't know who he is without that prison cell to define him. Once a Marine, always a Marine."

"*Semper Fi*," they said in knuckle-bumping unison.

"You've been hanging around those Navy SEALs too long. You need a haircut."

"I just got a hair—"

"Luke!" Cait screamed from the bathroom, and both brothers came running.

Lucky reached her first. "Cait, what's wrong?" She'd changed into her black dress and was standing over the sink.

"Luke's ring…" She barely choked out the words.

"Turn off the water," he said, doing it himself. "Do you have any tools?"

"No, but Mrs. Pèna does."

Lucky steered her toward the toilet seat. "Stay put. Watch her," he said to Bruce, dashing out.

He was back in less than a minute; the landlady had stared after him as he took the stairs two at a time. Lucky crawled under the bathroom sink with the wrench and removed the S curve section of pipe. He turned it over in his palm and her engagement ring fell out.

He gave it to her, thinking that would make her happy. She closed her fist over it and sank to the floor to bawl her eyes out.

She sat with her back against the tub and her forehead to her raised knees. The black skirt of her dress covered her to the ankles. Her bare feet poked out beneath.

After a few moments, her heart-wrenching sobs subsided.

Lucky was no good at this. He crouched beside her, his hand hovering over her hair, thinking he should be able to soothe away her tears somehow. Out of the corner of his eye he caught sight of his brother's curious scrutiny and sank back against the tub beside Cait.

He looked to Bruce for help, but his brother just shrugged.

Lucky heaved a sigh. "It's okay, Cait," he said. "You still have the ring. Why don't you put it back on and you'll feel better."

"My fingers are too fat," came her muffled response.

"Let me see."

She opened her left fist and he took the ring. Without looking up, she turned her hand over. Her fingers didn't look fat, they looked delicate and graceful. He hesitated over her ring finger, then slid her diamond-and-emerald engagement ring past the first knuckle to the second where it would go no farther.

She lifted her head to look at her hand. "See," she said. "It was too tight. It took a whole bar of soap to get it off. I wish

I'd never taken it off in the first place." She sniffled. Her face was blotchy and her makeup running from her tears. His chest tightened.

He was pretty sure the whole-bar-of-soap thing was an exaggeration. But the ring wasn't going back on, at least not until after the baby was born.

Lucky reached around his neck and slipped off his dog tags. "This is just a temporary fix," he offered, unclasping it and sliding the ring down the chain. "I'm sure you have a much nicer chain to wear." He slipped it on over her head, and she lifted her hair over it. His brother's ring and his dog tags nestled together against her heart.

She wrapped him in a hug right there on the floor and gave him a wet peck on the cheek. "Thank you, Calhoun."

Lucky cleared his throat. "I've got to put this sink together so I can get the pipe wrench back to Mrs. Pèna." He turned his attention to replacing the S curve.

"I'll take it back," Bruce volunteered. "I, uh, just remembered something I have to do.... Can I get a rain check on dinner and a movie, Cait?"

"I thought Calhoun was leaving after this weekend?"

They both looked at Lucky. Caught in the middle, he shrugged. He didn't want to leave Cait in her condition, yet he couldn't keep pushing the date back indefinitely.

"Cait, when's the last time you had any real fun?" Bruce asked. "Why don't the three of us take a road trip. We could go to Vegas—"

"Not Vegas," Lucky said.

"Then Napa. Somewhere."

"She's carrying around a baby on her bladder. She doesn't need to be taking any road trips right now."

"It was just a thought," Bruce said. "I gotta get going." He helped Cait to her feet. And then he did something Lucky had only dreamed of doing. He put both hands on her abdomen. "Hey, Peanut." He bent down to talk to Cait's baby bump. "How you doing in there? It's Uncle Bruce. Gotta go, but I'll be back." He looked up at Cait. "Don't be sad. Luke's not gone, Cait. He's just gone on ahead."

"That's the nicest thing anyone has ever said to me," Cait said, giving Bruce a hug. He squeezed her back, and Lucky felt something for his brother he'd never felt before.

Jealousy.

CAIT WALKED BRUCE TO THE DOOR, and they spent a few more minutes saying goodbye before she closed it behind him. "I think I scared him off." She sniffed back the last of her tears.

"He's not that easy to scare off." Calhoun studied her from her bedroom doorway. More of his tattoo was visible under the shirt he wore over a T-shirt, but not enough to give it away.

"Are you sure? Raccoon eyes can be very intimidating," she said, dabbing at her face. "Waterproof mascara can only hold up for so long...."

He stepped back into her bathroom and returned with a wrung-out washcloth.

"Come here," he said, and he began to wash her face as though she was a little girl. She closed her eyes and let him.

She'd made some important decisions over the past three days. The first was not to name her baby after her husband. This baby needed his own name, one that didn't cause conflict for the man who'd given her such a precious gift. The second was the house. She no longer planned to sell it. She planned to move into it.

When he stopped washing her face, she opened her eyes again. They stared at each other for an instant before breaking the bond. She clenched her fist around his dog tags and Luke's engagement ring. She didn't want another chain. She wanted this one to carry the reminder of the other Luke in her life.

"Look at us," she said. "All dressed up and no place to go. Do you still feel like dinner and a movie? Since this is the last weekend in California for both of us."

"YOU'RE TALKING NONSENSE, CAIT," Lucky said for the tenth time that evening. He'd taken her to the Gas Light district in San Diego for a nice dinner, followed by a movie—some chick flick he'd normally find hard to watch, made unbearable after the bomb she'd dropped.

She was moving to Colorado.

She'd hushed him throughout the opening credits when he'd tried to talk sense into her. "What about your lease?"

"Month to month. I was on a waiting list to move into a two-bedroom after the baby was born. But why should I wait when I own a two-bedroom house?"

"In another state!"

"Shh," some guy behind them said, and Lucky gave the guy a dirty look. The movie hadn't even started yet. Cait reached over and squeezed his hand to keep him quiet throughout the rest of the movie previews. It worked, because all he could think about was how right, and how wrong, it felt to hold her hand.

Now they were on some walking tour of every place she and Luke had ever been. It was well past midnight.

"Actually this is the first thing I'm doing that makes any sense," she argued. "Bruce was right. I need to get away from here."

He'd like nothing better than to get her away from here.

They were in a seedier part of town. Her vintage car was parked in a gravel lot under a broken streetlight, and they were headed for some dockside watering hole called Manny's. She'd be lucky if her hubcaps were the only things missing when they got back to her car.

"This is the place," she said, looking up at a neon sign that had seen better days and needed a few bulbs. "This is where Luke hung out with his buddies. Before we were married, of course."

Of course. A SEAL bar.

Great. He looked at the cluster of motorcycles parked close to the door, including a Fat Bob. At least they had good taste in bikes.

"Are you sure you want to go in there, Cait?"

"Just one Shirley Temple," she said. "I want to buy the room a round and see if they'll 'flame the bar' for me. Luke said some SEALs even write that traditional send-off into their wills."

He took a deep breath, probably his last—he was a Marine walking into a Navy SEAL bar—and reached for the door handle. His haircut would give him away as a jarhead.

He doubted she even knew the implication.

"You don't have to go in there with me if you don't want to," she said as he opened the door for her. Some guy came flying out and landed on his ass. He got up again and flew right back in.

Lucky pushed Cait behind him. "You'd better let me check it out."

"And miss a bar fight?"

"Stay behind me," he ordered. John Wayne would have been proud. "If there's any fighting going on we're not staying in there. Do you hear me?"

She agreed. They passed though a short hallway between the outer and inner doors. And then he was opening the inner sanctum to the Navy SEAL den.

There *was* a fight going on inside. As Lucky turned to get them back outside, he realized he knew one of the brawling SEALs.

"Bruce!" Cait said, just as stunned as Lucky was.

Bruce was limping in a small circle with six of the biggest guys in the room surrounding him. His fists were up. He was a mess, his shirt untucked and buttons missing.

It was clear nobody wanted to fight him. They were just trying to get a drunk and disorderly Navy SEAL–trained Marine under control. But they were also tired of getting in the way of his fists.

The guy they'd met outside wiped his bloody nose on his shirt sleeve. "Calhoun," he said to Bruce, "get your ass back to the barracks. Manny'll call you a cab."

Lucky decided the bar's namesake was the guy behind the bar in a wheelchair with a baseball bat in one hand and a phone in the other.

Bruce seemed to consider it for a moment.

The momentum of his circling slowed. He lowered his hands. Then he caught sight of Lucky and Cait and threw his head back and laughed. "Now you guys are in trouble." Bruce pointed right at Lucky. "My big brother's here and he's going to kick some Navy SEAL ass!"

Lucky had the attention of every SEAL in the place. Even if they didn't see their injured, drunk teammate as a threat, they immediately sized him up as one. At least ten more guys stood from their tables. And the pool players and the dart players in back stopped shooting.

Although he'd like nothing better than to teach these squids a lesson in hand-to-hand combat, he knew when he was outnumbered. Besides, he was with Cait.

He held up his hands. "I'm not here to cause trouble."

Cait was snug up against his backside. And he imagined, as eager as she'd been to witness a bar fight, she was probably having second thoughts about that right now.

"The lady here…" he didn't know if they could see her behind him "…just wants to buy a round in honor of her late husband, Luke Calhoun." As he'd hoped, the name sparked recognition. "My brother. *Bruce's brother*," he said, stating the obvious. "Then I'll take care of getting this idiot out of your hair—"

"Hey," Bruce protested.

"Ask them about flaming the bar," Cait said, now at his side.

The guy with the bloody nose nodded. The owner went back behind the bar and started lining up shots of whiskey. Chairs were set upright. Men in the back resumed playing pool.

Finally, Lucky could relax. A bit.

He nodded Cait toward the bar.

Lucky grabbed Bruce by the arm on the way. "Hey," Bruce protested again, "I just wanted to show 'em I still have some fight in me."

"You're not proving anything with all of this," Lucky said, forcing his brother onto a bar stool. "Stay out of trouble long enough for us to leave here in one piece."

"You're the only one of us leaving in one piece." Bruce laughed at the irony.

"Do you think I wouldn't trade places with you or with Luke if I could?" Lucky asked in a harsh rasp. He'd been the lucky one. That didn't mean he felt lucky.

Cait ordered her Shirley Temple and slid her credit card across the bar to pay for the drinks. The guys raised their shot glasses in salute. "To Luke Calhoun," someone said.

"To Luke," Bruce repeated, throwing one back before Lucky could stop him. "What?" Bruce challenged. "I can drink to my dead brother."

Lucky was still scowling at him when Cait tapped him on the shoulder. She held out a shot glass for him. He shouldn't. He was already running on adrenaline. The barkeep had cleared the bar and was pouring a line of whiskey down the center. Lucky could see the other burn marks left behind. And he didn't want to insult her.

"To Luke," he said, just as the barkeep lit one end of that whiskey trail on fire. The flame roared down the line. Throwing back his shot, Lucky felt the burn all the way down his throat. There was a time when he would have choked on those words rather than pay tribute to his half brother. "Come on. Let's get out of here," he said to Cait, setting his shot glass down on the table.

But, transfixed by that flame, she watched until the fire burned out. He stopped his brother from stealing any more shots and they left with Bruce tripping over his one good foot.

Cait's car and her hubcaps were still intact. "Are you okay, Bruce?" she asked.

His brother didn't deserve her sympathy. "If you have to puke you do it outside the car," Lucky said.

Bruce relied heavily on both of them to make it up the stairs to his barracks room. "You smell pretty, Cait."

He had an arm around each of them. But Lucky shouldered the burden of his brother's weight.

"Don't breathe on her," he warned. "You stink." Bruce looked at him, and Lucky had to turn away. His brother's breath was strong enough to knock a man out. "How much have you had to drink tonight?"

"Not enough," Bruce answered. "You two make a cute couple," he said, looking from one to the other.

"You're drunk. You don't know what you're saying. So just keep your mouth shut," Lucky snapped. "Give Cait your room key so she can open the door."

His brother was quartered by himself in a room usually reserved for someone of a much higher rank. They stepped into a small seating area with a TV. Through two open doors, they could see a small bedroom and a small bathroom.

"How do you rate? Your room's better than mine."

"It'll only cost you an arm or a leg." Bruce laughed.

"Say good night to Cait," Lucky said.

"Thanks for the ride, Cait." Bruce staggered off to his bedroom and closed the door behind him.

The front door was still open. Cait set Bruce's keys down on a nearby end table. "Well, that was some memorable last stop. Is he going to be all right?"

"I'll stay with him tonight," Lucky said, eyeing the serviceable couch and chairs, which looked like something you might find in a waiting room. Or a military barracks. "Can you make it home all right?"

"I'll be fine."

It was almost 0200 hours according to his watch. And he didn't want her driving home alone this late at night. He didn't think her staying here was an option, either.

Unless he kicked Bruce out of his bed.

They heard a loud thunk from the other room.

Lucky opened the door to investigate. "What the—"

Bruce was passed out on the bed, his pants down around his ankles. Seeing that adjustable pole where his brother's leg should have been came as quite a shock. He knew the leg was gone. He'd seen that kind of battlefield injury before. But the distance between them these past months had kept it from registering.

His brother's leg was really gone.

He picked up the half-empty tequila bottle from the floor. Beer. Whiskey shots. Tequila.

Not necessarily in that order. What else had Bruce been indulging in tonight?

Cait was already pushing past him to gather the prescription bottles spilling out of his brother's overnight bag.

For a moment, while Cait read the labels, opened bottles and counted pills, Lucky knew real terror unlike any he'd ever known in war. It didn't take her more than a few seconds to assess the situation. The look on her face…

"What and how many?" He'd already flipped open his cell phone to dial 911.

"None."

It took a moment for what she'd said to register and for him to close his cell. "Then what's wrong?"

"He hasn't taken *any* of these pills."

"You said that."

"I mean none! In the three months since these prescriptions were last filled, he hasn't taken a single pill. These are some heavy-duty controlled substances. Pain meds. Sleep aids. Your brother is an amputee. He needs these medications…for now."

Lucky was still trying to digest what she was saying.

"I've seen this before," she continued. "Someone so afraid of addiction, they quit their meds and wind up self-medicating. And addicted to something else."

She didn't have to point out the tequila bottle. He knew what she was talking about.

She took Bruce's limp wrist in her hand and checked his pulse. "I didn't mean to scare you. He's fine at the moment. I'm not a doctor, but we know he's not mixing drugs and alcohol, so that's not the concern here."

She was talking to him but looking at Bruce. "Have a talk with him when he's sober. And if you need to, call his doctor. Or I will if you want me to." She spared him a glance. "It's better for him to be on controlled meds under supervision than to self-medicate with alcohol."

"I'll take it from here and get him undressed."

She didn't move. "He looks a lot like Luke in his sleep." And again Lucky felt a surge of jealousy.

"Go home, Cait. Get some rest."

She hesitated at the door. "You should take off his leg. I don't imagine it's too comfortable to sleep with. He's an above-the-knee amputee, so it's a harness," she explained. "I did my pharmacy internship at a hospital."

"I got it," he said. "Good night, Cait."

CHAPTER SEVEN

CAIT WAS SURPRISED TO FIND both brothers on her doorstep early the following morning. Well, before noon, anyway.

She hadn't been up long herself and was only wearing an untied Oriental silk robe over her pajama pants and Luke's T-shirt.

They were in workout clothes. T-shirts and basketball shorts. The sleeves and collar of Calhoun's T-shirt were missing. She got her first real look at that tattoo, an intricate Celtic design that appeared to cover his shoulder and then some.

"Did you two run all the way here?" Their dripping sweat being her first clue.

"More like hobbled," Bruce said, bent over at the waist. He looked a little green around the gills. Lucky elbowed him in the ribs. "I wanted to apologize for my behavior last night. We brought you bagels." He held up the bag.

She opened the door wide and let them inside. "Bruce, if you need help—"

"I just got carried away last night, that's all."

She hoped that was true. She exchanged glances with Calhoun. "I know your physical pain is real. Emotional pain is, too," she said, thinking of the fiancé who'd deserted him. "A doctor can prescribe something for that."

If a doctor could prescribe something for a broken heart, Cait would have taken that drug herself a long time ago. She'd really like to know who this high school sweetheart was who'd broken Bruce's heart. Did she live in Colorado or California? Because if Cait ever ran into her…

"No drugs," he said, shaking his head. "No booze, either. And especially no doctors. Cait, I got all the lecture I needed from the big guy here." He tilted his head in Calhoun's direction. "And a workout to boot. Mind if I use your bathroom to puke?"

Bruce disappeared down the hall, and Calhoun followed Cait into the kitchen. She poured a round of orange juice while Calhoun got out plates and knives.

"He'll be okay," he said, joining her at the breakfast bar. "We had a talk. Actually, we're here to talk you out of moving to Colorado."

"*You're* here to talk her out of it," Bruce said, coming into the kitchen. "I think it's a great idea." Bruce grabbed a bagel, and Calhoun gave up his seat to lean against the counter.

"Okay, *I'm* here to talk you out of it. Do you think it's wise to make a cross-country move in your condition?"

"Colorado is not across the country," she argued. "It's only halfway across the country from California."

"She's right," Bruce agreed between bites. He was too macho to take the unoccupied stool right away, but he worked his way over to it now and sat down. Maybe there was something to be said about the way guys—*brothers*—communicated.

"But this week? What about your stuff?"

"I'll put everything in storage. I know how to travel light. I was a Navy wife, remember?" Well, it sounded good, anyway.

"What about your job?"

"I'm temping."

"What are you going to do when you get there? And how are you going to get there?" Calhoun persisted.

"Fly. And find a job. In that order," she snapped.

"Is that safe?" He looked at Bruce. His brother shrugged.

"I haven't reached my seventh month yet. I can still fly, and I can still find a job. I've had three days to think about this—" four now "—and you're not going to change my mind. What do you care? You're leaving."

"And if I stayed, would you stay?" he demanded.

"How long?"

"Until…the baby's born," he offered grudgingly.

"No." His attitude only reinforced her decision. She needed family. A support system for Peanut. Not some guy who argued for her to stay while he couldn't wait to leave. And Bruce had his own issues to deal with. He shouldn't have to put up with hers.

"What are you going to do about your car? Store it, too? And what happens when you get there and you need your car and your things?"

"Argh!" She was ready to pull her hair out. "You're relentless!"

She stood there with one hand on her hip and the other raking her sleep-tousled hair. "I'll call a moving company. I want to be happy and healthy and whole again. I don't want to look around every corner for Luke because it's someplace we've been.

"But I don't want to forget him, either. I want to be with people who loved him and still love him. I want to know what he was like as a boy so I have something to share with my son.

I want to know all those things about him that I never got the chance to learn.

"I'm moving to Colorado whether you like it or not!"

"Okay, then," he said, raising his voice above hers. "I'll drive you there. And then I'm gone."

"I don't want you to drive me. And quit looking at my boobs and my belly when you're talking to me." She stormed off to change.

"You are so busted." Cait heard Bruce chuckle as she slammed her bedroom door.

She jerked open her underwear drawer, grabbed a bra and panties. Then she opened and closed several more drawers looking for something to wear. She settled on a white tank top from the bottom drawer and black jumper from her closet.

Why was everything she owned black?

She was pregnant. She was just as happy about that as Marilyn was about her pregnancy.

She should be wearing bright colors. And pastels!

Catching a glimpse of the lighthouse in the distance, Caitlin laid everything out on the bed and moved to the French doors. Opening them, she leaned against the frame with her arms folded under her bust.

She'd miss that view. But that was the only thing she'd miss about this place. She closed her hand over the chain around her neck and stared out at the ocean.

A few minutes later, in her bathroom, she stripped down to those dog tags between her breasts. In her bathroom mirror, she regarded her naked form from all angles. "I do have great boobs," she said appreciatively.

Knowing him, he had probably been looking at his dog tags and wondering how he was ever going to get them back.

After a shower, she rejoined the Calhoun brothers in her kitchen. If it was a tight fit for one, it was an impossible fit for three, plus her big stomach.

"Okay," she said as she passed Calhoun.

"Okay, what?"

"You can drive me to Colorado."

CAIT DROPPED THE BROTHERS OFF at Camp Pendleton with the promise to pick Calhoun up in an hour outside his company headquarters. In the meantime, fueled by her earlier wardrobe disaster, she went shopping at the base exchange.

She found so many cute maternity clothes she bought one of everything that fit. The sticker shock didn't hit her until the grand total at the register.

Even at Navy Exchange prices, the spree cost a small fortune.

She'd earned it. And she deserved it. After months of sacrifice, that was her new motto. She handed over her debit card with a flourish. Gathering her overstuffed bags, she hurried out the door and toward her car.

She made it back to Calhoun ten minutes after the hour. Then waited another five before she got out of the car and entered the building to look for him.

There was a quartermaster on deck. Or whatever they called them in the Marine Corps.

"I'm looking for Master Sergeant Luke Calhoun Jr." Her voice echoed through the halls. The young private pointed her in the right direction, and Cait followed the polished tile to his polished nameplate beside a door that was ajar.

Somewhat surprised he even had an office, she knocked.

"Enter," he answered in an official-sounding voice. He was wearing his uniform again. Probably for the last time.

"It's me."

"I've just about finished packing," he said. He put a plaque in the box he had nearly filled, then looked around at the empty walls and desk. "Can't forget this." He shifted his box of files to one arm and reached for a long, rectangular case.

She couldn't imagine what it held.

"That's it," he said, ushering her out with one last look behind him. He shut off the lights and closed the door, then removed his nameplate and added it to the box.

"That was a desk," she said, still amazed.

"Didn't use it much."

She stopped to read the wall opposite the door on their way out. "You're, like, the senior noncommissioned officer for the whole company."

She was as surprised as he had been when he'd discovered she was a licensed pharmacist with the letters RPh after her name. Well, the letters MSGT in front of his must have meant something, too.

"Was," he conceded.

The private stepped forward to hold open the door, and Calhoun followed her outside.

"Can I get your keys?" he asked and she handed them over. "I just want to lock this in the trunk."

"The back seat is empty," she volunteered.

"I can't leave a rifle in the back seat."

"Rifle?"

He opened the trunk. "Clothes?" he asked, amused by the overflowing shopping bags.

"I didn't have anything to wear that wasn't black."

"WHERE'S CAIT?" BRUCE ASKED on Sunday when Lucky picked him up in the U-Haul.

"She's been shopping and packing since yesterday."

"When were you two going to tell me about the baby?"

Lucky glanced at Bruce, then back at the road. His hands tightened on the steering wheel. "What is it you think you know?" he asked evasively.

"It's not what I think I know. It's what I know. It's the way you look at her. And the way she touches her belly whenever she looks at you."

It was seventy-five degrees outside, but he felt a chill.

"And," Bruce continued, "it was that really lousy excuse you gave me to go meet her at CryoBank. So *are* you the donor?"

"You can't say anything to anyone."

"Why you?" Bruce asked.

"Why not me?"

"I'm better-looking." Bruce shrugged at the obvious. "Luke and I could've passed for twins as kids."

"That's because you're Irish twins. Same father, different mothers. Born weeks apart." That had never seemed to bother Bruce as much as it did Lucky.

"Which is why it would make more sense for her to ask me."

"Be glad she didn't," Lucky said, turning right into the storage facility.

"You two haven't…" Bruce ventured into personal territory as only a brother could.

"No, we haven't." Now, wouldn't that complicate things? He changed the subject. "I'm looking for number 168." He read the number Cait had written down. Lucky switched his attention to Bruce. "You and Luke may look alike, but you've never had to share the same name. You don't know what it's like to get an immunization twice because someone switched your medical records."

"Okay, okay. I've heard that story before. Don't you get tired of blaming him?"

"I'm not blaming him," Lucky said in a more subdued tone. He had, in fact, blamed Luke many times over. "This is more serious than my getting a booster shot. Cait got pregnant with my sperm. And Luke's got destroyed."

"Wow!"

"Yeah, wow."

"So you're going to be a father."

"No," he said. "I'm going to be an uncle. Same as you."

"I don't think it works that way."

"It works however Cait says it works. And that's why you can't say anything to anyone. Not even Cait."

The long silence in the truck cab was broken by Bruce pointing out her storage unit. "There it is...."

Lucky pulled up in front of Cait's unit. He got out of the truck and walked around back. He raised the door and his brother helped lower the ramp.

The only thing in back was his rifle case, a rented dolly, furniture pads, boxes and other moving supplies.

"Wouldn't it be smarter to pack up her apartment first?"

"Cait said she had more furniture in storage than in her apartment." He figured he may as well start with the unknown.

He didn't figure Bruce would be much help with the heavy lifting, so he'd included him, but he'd enlisted the help of Estes and Randall and expected them along any minute.

Lucky dug the key out of his pocket, then freed the padlock to raise the garage door.

"Man, you're gonna need a bigger truck."

Exactly what Lucky was thinking.

CAIT HAD NO IDEA HOW THEY'D managed to fit everything into one truck. Luke's motorcycle was secured across the back. And there was a trailer hitch for towing her car.

"Ready?" he asked.

She stood on the balcony of her empty bedroom, in her empty apartment, and looked out at the Old Point Loma Lighthouse one last time.

Calhoun had suggested a visit to the cemetery, but this was where she wanted to say her goodbyes.

She found no comfort in a graveyard.

"Ready," she said, putting on a brave front. "Just a quick trip to the bathroom." Who moved across the country pregnant?

And so began their road trip. She was becoming very familiar with the potty stops along the way. Her father had always said if you wanted to get to know someone, take a road trip with them. If that was the case, then she had to give Calhoun credit for his patience and thoughtfulness.

She called her father from the road.

"Hey, Daddy."

"Well, hey there, yourself."

"Sorry to bother you at work. I just wanted to let you know we're on the road."

"Now, who's *we?*" he asked. "The brother-in-law with the missing leg?"

"No, the other one," she said, leaning against the hood while Calhoun filled the gas tank.

"The one just back from Iraq? How do you know he's not some serial rapist?"

"Daddy!"

"Well, how do you?"

"Because he's not."

"Did you ever find out why he and Luke were on the outs?"

"It's complicated. He doesn't talk about it."

"When it's family, Caitie, it's always complicated."

"This move to Colorado is a good thing. I'll be near Luke's family. And I'll have my own house. Remember? I told you about it—the wedding present from Luke's father."

"The father he never mentioned. And you're on your way there with one of two brothers he never mentioned. Maybe you'd better let me talk to him," her father said.

"Don't you dare say anything accusatory," she said, hesitating to give Calhoun the phone. She'd been a late-in-life baby, and her father was getting on in years. From his button-down shirts to his bow ties, sometimes it seemed as if he was from another era. "He'd like to speak to you," she said as Calhoun finished pumping and hung up the nozzle.

"Sure." He wiped his hands on his jeans before taking her cell phone. "Yes, sir," he said. "I *do* have a valid driver's license."

Caitlin sighed heavily. She could almost hear her father's questions as he grilled Calhoun. *I'm sorry,* she mouthed.

He shook his head. It didn't seem to bother him at all.

"About 1100 miles. I've done it in fourteen. On a bike…. No, a motorcycle. This trip, twenty, twenty-four. Straight through…. Yes, sir," he repeated, grinning at something her father said. "She's a beauty."

Caitlin caught her breath as Calhoun held her gaze. Then he took a few steps back toward her Mustang up on the tow bar. He looked her car up and down.

"Restored her yourself?" He listened for a long time. "I will do that," he said, ending the call and handing back her phone. "Mrs. Mickleson needed her thyroid prescription filled."

"Thank goodness for Mrs. Mickleson's thyroid."

"So your dad's a pharmacist, too."

"Yeah, he owns his own drugstore. It's the only drugstore in Annapolis with its original soda fountain. I grew up wanting to be a soda jerk."

"Sounds like a nice place."

She shrugged. "Home was someplace I grew up wanting to leave. My dad worked long hours. I hardly ever saw him outside the store. When I wasn't at the store I was with my grandma. She was old and didn't get out much."

"But you didn't leave. Even after college."

"No, not until I met Luke. He was all those things I wasn't—adventurous…" She stopped there, not wanting to be reminded of all the things she missed about him.

"Why didn't you just go back?" he asked, meaning after Luke died even if he didn't say it.

She looked at the cell phone in her hands, then into his eyes. "But there's no going back, is there?" That applied to their situation as well as any. Caitlin excused herself to find a bathroom. When she came back out Calhoun was leaning against the hood of the truck. Caitlin held up the hubcap with the bathroom key attached and shrugged.

He laughed, which made her laugh.

Considering the gas station kept the bathroom under lock and key, and as picky as they were about that key, it wasn't all that clean. She'd learned to carry along her own toilet paper and sanitizing gel.

Calhoun had a bottle of cranberry juice waiting for her when she came out. "We're halfway home," he said, handing it to her. And he didn't once comment on how much faster that trip would be without her needing to stop every hour.

THE BLAST OF AN AIR HORN startled Cait out of a sound sleep. "What was that?" she asked as the headlights passed in the opposite direction. Lucky kept his focus on the road and the flashing red-and-blue behind him.

He pulled over to the shoulder as soon as it was safe.

Cait still looked confused and half-asleep. "Why is he stopping you?"

The officer pulled up behind him, got out and approached the U-Haul. Lucky rolled down his window.

"Have you been drinking tonight, sir?"

"No," Lucky answered, clearly sober. It was around last call, 0200 hours. But as far as he knew, Utah was a dry state. Must be the California plates.

"Driver's license and rental agreement for this vehicle, please." The Utah Highway Patrol officer shone his flashlight into the truck cab with his left hand while Lucky reached across Cait into the glove box for the rental agreement. The officer's right hand rested on the hilt of his make-my-day gun. "Do you have any weapons in this vehicle, sir?

Give me a break.

"Yes," he conceded. "I have a sport rifle locked up in back."

He'd just given the guy probable cause to open the truck. But he had nothing to hide.

"I'll need to see that registration, too."

Any pretense of politeness was gone as Lucky reached into his back pocket for his wallet. Slowly. He handed over his license, registration and all other pertinent papers to the officer.

He waited for the order to get out of the vehicle and place his hands on the hood. At the very least he expected he'd be opening up the back and taking a roadside sobriety test.

"Keep your hands on the steering wheel, sir, where I can see them," the officer said before heading back to his patrol car. This guy was by the book all the way.

Keeping his hands on the steering wheel, Lucky watched through his side mirror until the beam from the patrol car's headlights blinded him. It was late and only a few cars passed them on this stretch of the highway.

"What does he want?" Cait whispered, even though the officer wasn't within earshot.

He shrugged, but he had a hunch.

They'd been making good time until now, despite the frequent stops, which had become less frequent once Cait had fallen asleep. They'd left California at noon, hit the usual traffic snarl in the city, but managed to get ahead of rush hour as he'd continued along I-15 North.

They were west of the Utah/Colorado state line on I-70 East. Once he hit Grand Junction, Colorado, he'd be another five, maybe six hours from the home he hadn't seen in fifteen years.

The officer returned, more relaxed. His hand rested on his belt buckle, not his weapon. "Do you know why I pulled you over, sir?" he asked, handing back Lucky's license and registration.

He could guess.

He just wanted to take his lumps—in the form of a ticket—and get back on the road.

"You were driving down the middle of the road with your lights off."

"Yes." He realized he'd been busted the minute he saw the flashing red-and-blue lights.

"Saw some action in Iraq myself. How long you been back?"

"A week," he said, rounding up.

The guy nodded in complete understanding. "I can vouch for the fact that there are no IEDs between here and the Colorado state line. Been back a year and I still look at every piece of roadside trash wondering if it's going to explode."

They talked some more about the trafficking of drugs and illegals along that stretch of I-70, but Lucky felt Cait's growing impatience beside him.

"I'm going to let you off with a warning. Keep to your own lane. And keep your lights on." He rapped on the driver's-side door. "Welcome home."

LUCKY'S HANDS WERE STILL shaking when he pulled over in Grand Junction to fill up. That little incident in Utah was exactly the reason he shouldn't be the guy responsible for her welfare.

He could have killed somebody tonight.

He could have killed Cait. And Peanut.

Instincts that kept him alive in Iraq weren't the same ones necessary to function in a society where his biggest concern was how much he was going to pay for this tank of gas.

He wished she'd say something.

"I think we should stop for the night," she said.

Anything but that.

"I'll be right back," he muttered. For once Cait didn't get out of the truck right away. He went inside the quickie-mart to pay for his gas and to grab something with caffeine in it and a cranberry juice for Cait.

"Pump number three," he said, securing the lid on his large cup of coffee. Her juice was sitting on the counter when he said something really stupid. "And a pack of Lucky's."

He added a pack of gum to his impulse purchase.

He'd just smoke one.

Craving that calming effect, he lit up right outside the store. Cait must have gone to the restroom after all. He hurried his cigarette along so he'd be done before she came back out.

The truth was, coming home felt a lot like unfinished business. He needed a couple of drags just to put it all in perspective. The last time he'd smoked a cigarette was the night he'd left.

He hadn't looked back since.

He put out the cigarette and headed back to the U-Haul.

That was the night he'd burned his father's business to the ground. "Welcome home."

CALHOUN PULLED INTO THE Best Western parking lot. "I'll just be a minute," he said. A few minutes later he came back with two room keys. "The only vacancies they had were on the second floor. Hope you don't mind." He handed her a key.

"I'm pregnant, not handicapped."

He grabbed their overnight bags from the trunk of her car and his rifle case from the U-Haul, then double-checked the padlock. "I don't leave it out of my sight," he explained about the rifle case, "unless I know it's secure."

He saw her to her room, then disappeared into the one next door. After she freshened up, she changed into her pajamas and got ready for bed.

Despite the late hour, she had a hard time falling asleep. Why was he driving down the middle of the road with no lights on? Well, parking lights. She wasn't going to get any sleep until she had an answer. She wasn't going to get an answer until she asked the question.

Peeking out her window, she saw Calhoun leaning against the railing outside. He'd been tense since they'd been pulled over by the highway patrol, but that tension had increased since crossing the Colorado state line.

She stepped outside. Took a deep breath and moved to the rail. The balcony overlooked a swimming pool illuminated by floodlights. It shone a brilliant wavy blue against the black night.

He saw her but didn't say anything.

He still wore his jeans and a T-shirt.

She noticed the glow from his cigarette. "You smoke?"

"An old habit I thought I'd kicked," he said, taking one last drag and snuffing it out.

"Did you know smoking kills the lining of your lungs, tiny hairlike follicles called—"

He cut her off with a look that said he didn't want to hear it.

"You should try deep-breathing exercises. They release chemicals in the brain to calm you down and make you feel better without smoking."

He didn't say anything. She supposed that sounded like a lecture, too. Caitlin peeled at the chipping paint on the wrought-iron rail, then made herself leave it alone before she caused somebody extra work.

He was a grown man, and she didn't want to lecture him, either, so she tried a different tactic. "I couldn't quite figure out Bruce's connection to Luke's team. He wouldn't tell me. But he did mention that in 2003 he was one of a select group of eighty-eight Marines to train and serve with Navy SEALs."

Calhoun continued to stare straight ahead and she continued with her story.

"I guess he and Luke went to rival high schools and had to learn to work together in BUD/S.

"It didn't take me long after that to figure out why he was avoiding me. He lost his leg in the same blast that killed Luke. Except he didn't want me to find out because he knew I'd have questions." She stopped to look at him until he was looking back at her. "I bullied him into giving me answers."

Somewhere in the distance a door opened and closed.

"Bruce says there's an unmistakable pop when an IED explodes. But you already knew that. You don't have to explain to me why you were driving down the middle of the road. My husband was killed by a roadside bomb. But then, you already knew that, too." Her voice was husky as she said, "I bet your men felt really safe with you, Calhoun."

She saw everything she needed to in his eyes.

She sidled down the rail until she was right beside him. Then she took his hand and placed it right over Peanut's foot. She watched the wonder on his face as they waited for another kick.

All those hard lines softened.

"I feel really safe with you. Good night," she said, backing toward her room. She paused at the door. "Don't beat yourself up about it. Even the officer didn't give you a ticket."

CHAPTER EIGHT

CAIT, IN HER BABY ON BOARD T-shirt and shorts, compared the houses on the block to the picture in her hand. "Is that it?" she asked eagerly.

"That's it," Lucky confirmed. It was hard not to be excited for a woman who looked for a man's strengths and not his weaknesses. And while he hadn't forgiven himself for last night, she had.

Now if only he could live up to her expectations without letting her down again.

Lucky pulled into the gravel driveway, if you could call the two weeded ruts a driveway, and stopped at the side of the house in front of a detached garage. The garage doors opened on hinges like a shed. A For Sale sign leaned up against one of those doors, evidence of how quickly the house had been taken off the market. Less than a week ago.

The house itself was a simple rectangular floor plan.

Two bedrooms, one bath. A thousand square feet.

A fresh coat of exterior paint. White with black trim.

Cait dug out her key. As soon as he stopped the U-Haul, she sprang from the truck to the side porch to do the honors. The porch was little more than two steps and a concrete slab with wrought-iron handrails and grillwork. Lucky followed her up those two steps. More wrought iron supported the shingled triangle that extended from the roof.

He couldn't remember anyone ever using the front door. It was always the side door. "I'm so nervous," she said. "Look, my hands are shaking. I can't even fit the key to the lock. Here, you do it." She gave him the key and he opened the door for her. She stepped into the kitchen while he flipped on the light switch.

The interior had a fresh coat of white paint, as well.

She worried her full bottom lip as she ventured farther into the house, the living room, the two bedrooms. The bathroom. All small. She opened doors and looked into drawers and cupboards. There was a laundry room/back porch add-on off the kitchen and a big backyard that needed attention.

"I'm sorry it's not what you expected," he said when they wound up back in the kitchen. It was exactly as he'd expected. Only smaller than he remembered.

"It's perfect," she pronounced. "It needs some color, but with a coat of paint and furniture... Can we start bringing it in?"

"If we're going to paint, we should do it before you move the furniture in," he suggested. Of course, she wasn't going to be painting or moving furniture. He was.

What was his plan? Drive her here and leave.

He added painting and unloading to the list.

It was already late afternoon, and they'd just driven how many hundred miles? "First things first," he said. "How about we go find a bed for the night and some help for tomorrow?"

LUCKY KNEW WHERE TO FIND BOTH. He just didn't know how welcome he'd be after fifteen years.

He thought about calling ahead, but he didn't think that would make this homecoming any less of a shock.

Less than a mile in distance, he pulled up to the curb of his mother's and stepfather's/uncle's house. He turned off the ignition and sat in the truck a moment to collect his thoughts. He had no idea what he was going to say to them. It wasn't as if he never spoke with his mother, but...

"Why don't you wait in the car," he suggested to Cait.

Getting out, he closed the truck door and made his way to the front. The place looked the same. Same basketball hoop over the garage. Same crack in the driveway. Same landscaping. Same color brick and neutral siding.

If the other house represented his early years, this house represented all the years that followed.

He rang the bell and waited.

A few seconds later the door opened and Keith stood there dressed in team colors with a basketball under his arm. He was a whole hell of a lot taller than Lucky remembered. Keith looked past him to the U-Haul at the curb. "Is that Cait?" he asked.

Lucky looked over his shoulder to see Cait waving. She'd gotten out of the truck. Probably had to go to the bathroom.

"Yeah," he answered.

"Are you Lucky?" his brother asked.

Lucky swallowed the lump in his throat. "Yeah."

"I kind of remember you from that trip to Disneyland in California when I was seven."

"I remember you."

"I'm taller than you," bragged the teen.

They weren't exactly on even footing here—the kid was

up a step—but he'd give him that. Lucky had about fifty pounds on him, though.

"You kind of look like dad," Keith added. Meaning Keith's dad. Lucky's uncle.

"Yeah, yeah, I do." They could be standing here all evening going through a checklist of similarities and differences. "Hey, is Mom home?" he asked.

"Mom!" Keith called over his shoulder. "Lucky's here! Gotta go. You should come to one of my games." He scooted past Lucky and out the front door. Keith waved to Cait as he headed to the '90 Thunderbird in the drive. The car was as old as the kid.

"Ohmigod, ohmigod!" his mother screamed as soon as she spotted Lucky standing in the doorway. "John, come here!"

Lucky felt his hackles rise and rolled his shoulder as soon as she mentioned his uncle. As a teen, he hadn't always been respectful of the man and was unsure of his welcome. But Lucky had always liked him a lot better than he liked Big Luke. It's just that he'd been about ten when he'd discovered his mom and his paternal uncle were sleeping together. They were married a short while later.

Not that there *was* anything wrong with that. They weren't related except by marriage, a marriage that had ended badly long before their affair had started—just like it would be if he and Cait… Lucky stopped that thought in its tracks.

It felt wrong to think it, let alone want it.

His mother wrapped him in her arms.

"I can't believe my eyes," she said, hugging him to her breast. He felt an ache in his chest when he hugged her back.

Finally, she stepped back to get a good look at him and he got a good look at her. She was older, of course. A little heavier. She still wore scrubs and an ID badge that said she still worked at the VA hospital. "John, come here!" she hollered again.

His uncle met them at the door. Lucky acknowledged him with a nod. His uncle offered his hand and they shook. John was the opposite of Big Luke. Quiet, reserved. Sincere.

So Lucky believed him when he said, "Welcome home."

"Who's that?" His mother had turned her attention to the pregnant woman and the U-Haul.

"That's Cait," he said.

His mother looked to his uncle, then back to him. "Luke's widow-bride Cait?" she asked.

FINALLY, CALHOUN WAVED HER TO the door. He'd just saved her from having to knock on a neighbor's door to use their bathroom.

She was nervous and that didn't help.

"Hi," she said to John, whom she recognized from the funeral.

"This is my mother, Evelyn," Calhoun said.

"Hi," Cait said again. "May I use your bathroom?"

"Yes, of course. Come in," his mother said as if just realizing they were still standing on the threshold.

"Top of the stairs," John said, giving her directions.

When Cait came out of the bathroom, Calhoun was standing at the top of the stairs with her overnight bag. "What a terrible first impression I make," she said.

"Don't worry about it." He showed her to a room with bunk beds across the hall. "This was my and Bruce's room." It looked as if it had been semi-converted to storage space, but other than that it looked like a boys' room.

There were a lot of basketball and motocross trophies lining the walls. She took one down. Luke Calhoun Junior. "You told me Luke was a dirt rider," she accused him. "You never told me you were."

He shrugged. "Must have slipped my mind."

She put it back and did a complete turn of the room, taking it all in. "Where are you sleeping?"

"On the couch," he said. "The plan is dinner after Keith's game in half an hour. Mom said to tell you if you're tired, don't feel obligated. She can fix you something now."

"I'm fine. I'd like to go to the game."

THE CROWD ROARED IN THOSE FINAL seconds of the Englewood versus Alameda game. She'd been torn between teams when Calhoun informed her that Luke had played for Alameda High.

She'd tried cheering for both. But in the end she was rooting for Keith. He'd played his heart out on that hardwood and scored a three-pointer from midcourt to win the game by one point.

"That was exciting, wasn't it?" She didn't know anything about basketball. Would her son have the basketball gene? Would Calhoun be attending any of those games? Calling out the official on those bad calls?

Why had he stayed away from his family for so long?

"Did you say something?" he asked, leaning in closer to her.

"I just said it was an exciting game," she said, raising her voice to be heard above the crowd this time.

"Great game," he agreed, taking her hand to help her navigate the bleachers and the crowd. Their hands were still locked when they stepped outside, waiting for John to pull around in the Explorer.

March was the snowiest month in Colorado, or so she'd heard. There wasn't any snow on the ground, although they'd seen some coming over the Rockies.

"Cold?" Calhoun tucked their hands into his jacket pocket. She hadn't thought to buy a new maternity coat and was wearing another of his old field jackets, so they were a matching pair. Except his old jacket was much bigger on her.

"I don't know which one I like best." Evelyn was trying to decide between two team spirit shirts when she joined them.

Caitlin tugged her hand back and into her own pocket.

Calhoun didn't seem to notice. Something that had felt so right just a few moments ago no longer felt right.

"Cait, do you have a preference?" his mother asked. She pointed to the one she liked and his mother ended up giving it to her. "Just in case Lucky brings you to another game. Besides, if you don't want to wear it in public it makes a good nightshirt."

John pulled up and they all piled into the Explorer.

Keith and his friends were driving themselves. They all met up at a sports bar that catered to families. Calhoun's parents didn't ply him with questions; they just accepted him and included her. She really liked that about them.

Keith dragged Calhoun off to a hoop-shooting contest to see who could win the most tickets. And Evelyn excused herself when her cell phone rang—it was soon clear Aunt Dottie was on the other end. "Yeah, she's here," Evelyn said, moving away from the table.

That left Caitlin and John alone at the table.

Caitlin happened to glance up at one of several TV monitors tuned to different channels just as a commercial came on. And there, right on screen in front of her, was Big Luke.

Big Luke wore a cowboy hat and a rawhide jacket with a fringe. "Come on down! For the best wheelin', dealin' around! It's Calhoun Cycles! South of Hampden on Broadway…"

And then he rode off on his hog, at least that's what she thought a motorcycle like that was called, into the sunset. It could be a Fat Bob for all she knew. But in those thirty seconds of sound bites—between the zoo animals and the sunset—he'd flashed an image of Luke.

Her dead husband, Luke.

In place of a ten-gallon hat he wore a combat helmet. A proud American, flag-waving father with a hand over his heart in tribute to the Navy SEAL son he'd lost in Iraq. He even shed a tear and claimed the uniform on display in his showroom was Luke's.

Not unless Nora Jean had given it to him.

The tear wasn't all that real, either.

Big Luke never even mentioned he had two other sons.

Both had served in Iraq. One had lost a leg and still served in the Marine Corps. Excluding his brothers was no way to honor Luke. She felt sad for all three Calhoun boys and their broken homes.

"Never mind him," John said, noticing her distress. "Evelyn gets real irate, too. We usually just change the channel."

Calhoun came back with bragging rights and the most tickets. He slid into the booth next to her, looking as happy as she'd ever seen him. She was glad he hadn't seen the commercial. Why did his father treat him as if he didn't exist?

CAITLIN WOKE UP AROUND MIDNIGHT and couldn't fall back to sleep. Maybe it was being in a different time zone. Maybe it was just the excitement of having a place she could call home.

They were going to Home Depot tomorrow to pick out paint. Calhoun had recruited his brother and uncle for the actual painting and moving. But in just one or two more days…Calhoun would be on the back of his bike and gone.

One minute she was picking out paint colors and moving into the place, the next she was thinking about his leaving.

Her stomach rumbled. Peanut was hungry.

She went downstairs to forage for cereal.

Calhoun was lying on the couch watching some old WWII movie on TV. He looked up as she passed through to the kitchen but didn't say anything. She brought her bowl into the living room, and even though there were plenty of seats, she sat on the end of the couch, making him move his feet.

"What is it we're watching?" she asked, between mouthfuls.

"Sands of Iwo Jima."

John Wayne played Sergeant Stryker, a battle-hardened Marine. Not unlike another Marine she knew.

"Gagon, a Navy corpsman, and two Marines, Hayes and Bradley, survived the battle and have a cameo in the movie," he said.

"Who?"

"Part of the six-man flag-raising team immortalized in the Pulitzer Prize–winning photo by Joe Rosenthal."

The Rosenthal picture had become the iconic image for the battle of Iwo Jima, if not the entire war, and was possibly the most reproduced photograph of all time. The Marine Corps War Memorial in Washington, D.C., depicted that famous incident in bronze.

"The flag used to recreate the scene is the actual flag raised on Mount Suribachi on February 23, 1945. It was on loan to the movie from the U.S. Marine Corps Museum in Quantico, Virginia. John Wayne gives it to Gagon as he instructs the men to hoist the flag. Just watch, it's near the end of the movie."

She finished her cereal, got up to put the bowl in the dishwasher, and when she came back Calhoun had stretched out his long legs. He moved again when she sat down.

Grabbing an accent pillow, she lay down on the opposite end. He had no choice but to adjust his position once again so that she had room. They waged their own tug-of-war over the knitted afghan until he gave up. But she wished he hadn't because now her feet were sticking out.

"Grenade. Hit the deck."

Cait watched as the platoon ran, following Sgt. Stryker's command, all except for one Marine, who was reading a love letter and had to be tackled to safety by Stryker when the grenade went off.

"You idiot. When are you gonna wake up? You wanna see that dame again, keep you mind on your work."

"You may not know this, boy," said another character in the movie, *"but you just got your life saved."*

She pushed her cold feet against Calhoun's T-shirt-covered chest. He took the hint and rubbed the warmth back into them. He continued to massage her feet absently, all the way to the end of the movie. He had no idea how good that felt to a pregnant woman.

"You didn't tell me John Wayne gets killed." She sniffed.

"That's what makes him the hero." His hands slowed on her feet. "Are you crying?"

"I'll be fine," she said, snuggling deeper into him.

LUCKY WOKE UP ON THE COUCH with Cait's feet burrowed under his T-shirt and an erection from all her other parts snuggled against his.

He extracted himself just as his mother was coming down the stairs. She gave him a disapproving glare, and he felt like he was in high school all over again.

He followed her into the kitchen in his gray gym shorts and T-shirt. She poured two mugs of coffee from a machine she must've had set to a timer.

"The widow-bride, Lucky." She *tsked* as she handed him a mug. "What are you thinking?"

"It's not like that," he said, keeping his voice low to avoid waking Cait.

She tilted her head to the side. "I always knew you'd find your way home with a pregnant girlfriend," she said in hushed tones. "But I at least thought the baby would be yours."

He couldn't even defend himself against that one.

"I'm just the driver," he whispered. "Then I'm gone again."

"Just who do you think you're kidding?" she whispered back. "I'm your mother! I see the way you two—" She stopped abruptly. "Oh my God," she said, sinking to a chair at the table. "The baby *is* yours."

Jeez, he couldn't fool Bruce and he couldn't fool his mother, even though he hadn't seen her in years. He had to get while the getting was good or soon the whole town would know his brother's widow carried his baby.

"It's not like that," he said harshly.

"You keep saying that," she accused him. "Then tell me what it is like."

"I'm the donor," he admitted for a third time.

"Oh my God! It's worse than I thought." She buried her head in her hands. "You mean to tell me Nora Jean has bragging rights to my *only* grandbaby?"

"*Please* keep your voice down," he begged. "I'm not the father. You're not the grandmother. And you can't tell anyone. Especially not Dottie."

"If you think I'm not going to tell your stepfather—"

"Don't call him that," Lucky growled. "Just because he's your husband doesn't make him my father. Step or not, he's my uncle."

"He's the only father you've ever known, and you will treat him with respect while you are in this house."

Some things never changed. John was the only father Bruce had ever known. But Lucky had known what it was like to have a real father once.

"I'm not trying to be disrespectful to John," he said. "You can't let Cait know that you know. As far as you're concerned, Cait's baby is Luke's baby. That's just the way it is."

Lucky rubbed the bridge of his nose.

His coffee mug, all but forgotten during this conversation, was the focus of his attention now. The deep hurt in his mother's eyes was worse than any accusation.

A sleep-tousled Cait stepped into the kitchen in her usual,

Luke's T-shirt and pajama bottoms. "Good morning," she said in a bright voice.

"Morning," Calhoun said. Cait couldn't help but notice he'd left off the *good*.

"I'm late for work," his mother said, getting up from the table and dumping the remains of her coffee in the sink before loading her mug into the dishwasher.

Cait couldn't help but notice the woman wouldn't look at her. She'd embarrassed herself by falling asleep on the couch with Calhoun.

That wasn't very good houseguest behavior.

She'd heard them arguing in hushed tones earlier. It must have been about her.

The woman probably thought she was trying to seduce her son. Cait put a hand to her stomach. As if she could seduce any man in her condition.

"Your mother hates me," she said, after Evelyn had left. She worked the dog tags around her neck.

"My mother doesn't hate you. She hates me."

AFTER BREAKFAST LUCKY BORROWED the keys to his uncle's old pickup. An hour later, with their cart full of cleaning supplies, they were arguing over paint chips.

Cait wanted a splash of color in every room.

"Do you realize how dark that's going to be on the walls? It's a small house, Cait. It'll seem even smaller once we move the furniture in."

"What about white ceilings and trim, and something neutral like this—" she held up her color choice "—in the living room and kitchen, and a shade darker in the bathroom and two shades darker in the bedroom…"

Neutral looked suspiciously like pink to him. Or at least in that girly color range. She insisted it was beige even though the paint chips read Flush, Blush and Blushing.

"What about something like this?" His hand strayed to the range of masculine hues. He picked out a smoky-blue with enough gray to keep it in the neutral zone.

"Oh," she said excitedly, "that would be perfect for the baby's room. Do you remember that blue-and-beige striped wallpaper I stopped to look at? And the teddy bear border? That would complement this color perfectly and the rest of the house."

The baby's room.

She was glowing in her pastel outfit, picking out her pastel paint. Absolutely radiant.

She kissed him on the mouth. Right in the middle of Home Depot. Not the kind of kiss that gave him time to stop and think. But a quick thank-you kiss. He supposed to the casual observer they looked like any other pregnant couple, instead of a couple with a secret.

"WHAT DO YOU MEAN I'D JUST BE underfoot?" Cait had asked later that afternoon.

"Just what I said," Lucky had argued. "You can't lift anything. You can't paint. I have plenty of help, and the whole house is going to be full of fumes…."

And that had put an end to that argument.

"You've been quiet," his uncle said. After a few hours of painting they were almost done. They just had the four walls in the living room left. Keith was doing the touch-up work on the trim in the bedroom. "Something on your mind?"

"Did she tell you to get me to talk about it?"

She meaning his mother. Lucky poured pink paint into a pan. Thank God he wasn't the one living here.

"She may have said something."

Of course she had.

"I'm just sticking around long enough to get Cait settled, then I'm out of here. Can we agree not to talk about it?" Lucky said from the opposite end of the room.

"We can do that."

John dipped his roller and concentrated on the white wall in front of him. His uncle was as much of a nontalker as he was. "Your mom sure likes having you home. She worries about you."

It had been too easy to spend those thirty days of military leave he earned each year doing something else, and with each passing year it had become more difficult to come home. The past four years, in and out of Iraq, he hadn't even had a choice.

When he'd opted out, he'd had over 120 days of leave on the books. He'd been paid for those four months in cash—almost sixteen thousand dollars.

That was a nice chunk of change, but it was worth the price—120 days he could have spent with his family.

"I did all right for myself, didn't I?" He'd meant the question to be rhetorical. But it sounded as if he was seeking his uncle's approval.

"You did all right."

He'd hate to think that after fifteen years as a Marine he'd amounted to nothing. But what did he have to show for it now? He was starting over from scratch with *nothing*.

Sure, he had a little money in the bank. And an idea of what he wanted to do with it. But he could have stayed in the Corps another five years until retirement and come out with a lot more security.

Before he'd started getting restless.

After his third tour. After Bruce and Luke.

After the chaplain put that bigger question to him, "Did you want to go home, son?"

Even though he'd said no—gotta be tough like a Marine, right?—deep down the answer had been yes.

"CAN I COME TO WORK WITH YOU?" Caitlin asked Luke's mother the next day. Hospitals could always use volunteers, and she needed something to occupy her time while the paint dried and the furniture was moved into her home.

Evelyn didn't say much on the way to the VA hospital, or once they arrived. She stuck Caitlin with bedpan duty. Not the most glamorous of jobs. And she saw enough old-man behinds to last a lifetime.

But it wasn't the old men in hospital gowns that bothered her. The facility was full of young men and women. Both in-patient and outpatient. Some in uniform. Some in civilian clothes. And, yes, some in hospital gowns or pajamas, reminding her that the number of dead in this war was eclipsed many times over by the number of wounded.

Here, too, her favorite ward was the amputee ward. In general the patients were young men and liked to flirt, making her feel good about herself. And if you looked them in the eye and didn't shy away from their injuries, they grew to love you.

They knew her as a young war widow. She'd been telling someone the story of her late husband's service and he'd told somebody else. And that person told somebody else. And pretty soon she was their hero. She'd tried to explain that she was nobody's hero, but they didn't want to hear it.

Her favorite patient on the ward was not a young man, but an old and crotchety one. A long-retired Marine. But as he liked to tell her, "Once a Marine, always a Marine." He'd come out of another war in one piece, but now he was fighting a losing battle with diabetes. First his foot. Then his leg.

"I see the doctor adjusted your insulin, Mr. Hobbs."

"You're not supposed to read my chart. You're just a candy striper."

"Is there even such a thing as a candy striper anymore?" She wasn't wearing the green hospital scrubs, but she was wearing her own cartoon-character ones. "I thought I mentioned yesterday I was a pharmacist."

"You want me to believe a pretty young thing like you is a doctor of pharmacology?"

"Yes," she said, fluffing his pillow. Though she should probably be careful about going around and saying that because she wasn't licensed in this state yet. As soon as she got her license she was going to apply.

"You got the one too high," he grumbled and she adjusted the pillows again. "I want to hear some more about that Marine. The brother-in-law."

"So you were listening."

"Ah." He blew her off. "*They* like you better a pregnant widow. I like you better a pregnant widow-bride."

"I told you, we're not getting married." She should never have confided in him about the baby. But the truth was, she needed to talk to someone.

She'd loved Luke with her whole heart.

But sometimes she felt like the biggest pretender in the world when it came to this baby.

"So you got that boy whipped and he left the Corps."

"He didn't leave the Marine Corps for me. And I certainly could never whip him. And neither could you."

"So he's a big strapping fellow."

"He's big," she admitted.

A commotion broke out around them as men began booing and throwing their rolled socks at the TV.

"We hate that commercial," Mr. Hobbs said.

Caitlin looked up in time to see Big Luke riding off into the sunset. "I hate that commercial, too."

"So you were saying he's a big strapping fellow. I retired a master sergeant myself," Master Sergeant Hobbs said, commanding her attention. "He treat you right?"

"He treats me right." Her stomach itched and she scratched it. Even though she shouldn't because it could cause stretch marks.

"Do you know if it's a boy or a girl?"

"A boy."

"Do you mind?" he asked, nodding toward her belly. The baby was very active of late. Sometimes her whole stomach seemed to churn.

"Sure," she said. At least he'd asked.

He put a hand on her. "That's a future Marine right there. I told you I breed English bulldogs, the unofficial breed of the Corps," he said in an aside. "When you and your husband get settled, I have a little something for you. A housewarming gift. What'd you say your husband's name was?"

"His name is Luke Calhoun Jr. And he's not my husband. He's my brother-in-law." And he's leaving. And I'm going to miss him. And it would be very wrong to want him to stay.

"Cait," Lucky's mother called to her from the doorway. "I need you to help pass out these trays."

After lunch Cait helped Evelyn administer meds by pushing a cart door to door. "I suppose you think you're way overqualified for this job," Evelyn said, studying her.

"No." She'd never expressed anything like that.

"Well, I can't let you give the patients their meds."

"I know."

"There *is* a job opening in the pharmacy if you're interested. Unless, of course, you're planning to spend time with the baby before going back to work."

Caitlin hadn't really thought about it. Who was going to take care of the baby while she was at work?

"John and I are always available to help with babysitting," Lucky's mother offered.

It was a very generous offer, considering Caitlin couldn't even figure out the woman's relationship to Luke. She wouldn't have been Luke's stepmother, even though Nora Jean would have been stepmother to Calhoun and Bruce—and Evelyn was their mother and Big Luke's first ex-wife.

And because of her relationship to John, that made her Luke's aunt. Aunt to your ex-husband's son. *Wow!* That must have been awkward. She didn't imagine the Calhoun clan had had too many family gatherings.

"I just realized, Evelyn, that you're my aunt by marriage. Is that right?"

"Kind of complicated, isn't it?"

Making other relationships even more complicated. "I want to apologize for this morning," Caitlin said.

"I don't know what you're talking about," Calhoun's mother said, pressing her lips together.

"Falling asleep on the couch with your son was not my intention." Did that mean Calhoun was her brother-in-law and her cousin-in-law? Was there such a thing as a cousin-in-law? "We were just watching an old John Wayne movie. There's nothing going on between us."

"He already explained that," Evelyn said. There was a sadness in her eyes as she forced a smile. "Let's finish up here so we can pick up Dottie and go see your new house." Aunt Dottie was also a nurse and worked on a different floor, in a different ward.

Evelyn started to say something else then changed her mind. "I want you to be sure and keep in touch when Lucky leaves."

CHAPTER NINE

CAITLIN KNEW HE WAS LEAVING. She just hadn't expected it to be so soon. When they pulled up to the curb in Evelyn's Explorer he was backing his motorcycle out of her driveway. Cait passed the bucket of KFC they'd picked up on the way home to Dottie and climbed out the back seat of the SUV.

Calhoun stopped at the end of the drive and took off his helmet while he sat astride his motorcycle with the engine running.

"You wouldn't leave without saying goodbye?"

"No," he said over the rumble of his bike. She felt a wave of relief.

He held his helmet in front of him and wore a black leather jacket over a T-shirt and jeans. "I just have some unfinished business I need to take care of." He met her gaze. "We'll talk when I get back."

"That sounds ominous."

He didn't deny it. The serious set to his mouth confirmed it.

"I'll be back soon." He put his helmet on and backed out. Caitlin stood watching as he roared up the street.

Evelyn stopped beside her. Turning to the other woman, Caitlin forced herself to smile. "It looks like they got a lot done around here."

Her car was parked on the street in front of the Explorer. The trailer hitch was up against the shed and the U-Haul wide open; only her extra bedroom set and dining room set and a few odds and ends remained in it. And she suspected that was because there wasn't enough room in the house.

John and Keith came out to greet them.

"I'm starving." Keith walked past with Calhoun's seabag on his shoulder and stopped to snatch a drumstick off the top of the bucket.

"Where do you want this, Cait?" he asked, indicating the bag.

"The laundry room is fine."

John couldn't wait to show off all their hard work and ushered the three women inside.

LUCKY REMOVED HIS HELMET AND put down his kickstand in front of Calhoun Cycles. He sat there a long minute before he climbed off his bike.

His father had expanded. The showroom was bigger and better than ever. He should have realized Big Luke would have gotten an insurance settlement and landed on his feet.

That didn't assuage his guilt. In fact it made him all the more guilty. Maybe even criminal.

The fire had started as an accident.

A careless flick of a cigarette.

A bucket of oily rags.

He'd been angry.

He'd spent the summer dreading his senior year. He liked high school well enough. But Luke would have been coming in as a freshman.

And that would have ruined everything. Just as it had in

elementary and middle school. Of course, those formative years had been made even more difficult by the hate he'd felt for Luke. Hate that had been misdirected. He'd badgered his mom to sign enlistment papers so he could join the Marine Corps before his eighteenth birthday. When she'd refused, he'd come here to convince Big Luke.

But he'd taken one look at the new sign going up, Calhoun & Son, and he'd felt sick to his stomach. He'd waited around long enough to know there was no *s* going up on the end of that sign.

Later that night he'd sat beneath that new Calhoun & Son sign on his motorcycle and smoked a cigarette. In those last few drags he'd kickstarted his bike and headed toward the exit out back.

He'd flicked his cigarette butt just as he'd cleared the garages. It must have landed in the bucket of rags because he saw the flash, heard the boom and skidded around in time to see the barrel of recycled oil catch fire.

He'd been a block away when the explosion had rocked the neighborhood. When he'd stopped to look back at those flames and that black cloud above the treetops, he should have felt something. But he'd felt nothing at all.

No guilt. No remorse. And there was no looking back after that.

His uncle had caught him coming in past curfew smelling like smoke from fire and cigarettes. But he'd been home only long enough to pack a bag. He'd convinced John to sign his enlistment papers. The truth was he'd been closer to his uncle than his father after his parents' divorce.

But once his uncle had married his mom and moved in, he hadn't been easy on any of them. At ten, Lucky had been too young to understand the relationship. As were the kids who persisted in teasing him and Bruce with choruses of "I'm My Own Grandpa."

He was big for his age, so the kids who picked on him tended to be two or three years older. He usually got the worst of those fights. And on the opposite end of the spectrum, in defense of his brother, he was seen as a bully.

Throw Little Luke into the mix and…well…he'd spent a lot of time in the principal's office.

By the time he was a teen he'd had other outlets.

Basketball. Motorcycles, motocross racing. And sex.

But he'd been out of control, rebelling against authority and discipline at every turn. Ironically, the very things he'd found in the Marine Corps that had made him the man he was today.

If there was a single reason he hadn't returned to Colorado in fifteen years, he was looking at it.

He got off his bike, ready to make peace with his past.

Big Luke had been cited for improper storage. He'd been deep in debt at the time of the fire and there'd been talk of arson. But that talk soon died down like flames to ash. Money exchanged hands, and the fire was labeled an accident.

Lucky had never told anyone where he'd been that night.

Though he didn't doubt Big Luke knew.

He walked in now as if he owned the place. At one time that had been his only ambition. He bypassed the eager sales staff for the empty reception desk outside his father's floor-to-ceiling glass office. The door was closed, but it wasn't soundproof, and Nora Jean was inside screeching at Big Luke.

"I want that commercial off the air.… It's tasteless."

All Big Luke's commercials were tacky.

Hitching up his pant leg, Lucky perched himself on the reception desk and prepared for a long wait.

"Hello, stranger," the receptionist said, coming around the corner from outside.

"Maddie," he acknowledged without getting up.

"Don't you mean Mom?" she teased, rounding the desk to have a seat. Opening the middle drawer, she put her smokes away and took out a pack of gum.

"I'm never going to call you that."

Maddie had been two years ahead of him in high school. They'd even dated, if you could call the back seat of her car a date.

She'd worn her leather too tight then, and she wore her leather too tight now. But he supposed the biker-babe image worked for her. After all, it had gotten her access to Big Luke's millions. And wasn't that why she'd broken up with him—because he hadn't had access to his father's money?

Like old times, she offered him a stick of gum. He shook his head. She took one stick for herself. He'd told himself his last cigarette was his last. But he could smell the secondhand smoke on her, and it made him edgy.

"I can let him know you're here if you want."

"He knows I'm here," he said, moving away from the desk. He'd caught Big Luke's eye the moment he'd walked up. And whatever Nora Jean's business, he didn't want to interrupt.

Nora Jean stormed out of Big Luke's office. She paused a few feet from him and did a double take. "What are you doing home?"

"Just passing through, *Mom*," he said, because he knew how much it irritated her to be reminded that she was his stepmother. Big Luke stood in his office door. The cut of his expensive suit couldn't hide the fact that he'd lost weight. But he still darkened the gray in his thick hair. Only now, instead of making him look younger, it made him look like a shadow of his former self. When the old man turned toward his desk, Lucky figured an open door was the closest he was going to get to an invitation. "Excuse me," he said to Nora Jean, who was still standing there with her mouth hanging open.

"What do you want?" the old man asked as he stepped into the office. Big Luke was older, his voice rougher with age and years of tobacco abuse. "A job?"

Lucky laughed without humor. "I didn't come here looking for work."

What Lucky wanted was what he'd always wanted—to be a Calhoun & Son. Hell, he didn't even need the sign, just the acknowledgment. He figured Big Luke owed him that much at least.

Lucky looked his father in the eye. "I was seventeen. It was an accident."

"Accident now, is it?" Big Luke's hacking cough took all the punch out of his sarcasm.

"I'm not here looking for your forgiveness. I'm here to try to find a way to forgive you. When I was four you treated me like I was disposable. When I was eight you stopped coming around. And as I remember it, alimony and child support payments were never on time." He glanced at Luke's military picture above his father's desk. "You had a new family. A newer business. I wasn't worth your time. But I forgive you."

"*You* forgive *me?*" Big Luke said, dumbfounded. "The only

reason you're not in jail is because I refused to press charges against my own son."

"Thank you for that." And he didn't mean about the not pressing charges. It was the first time in a very long time that he remembered his father calling him *son*.

He nodded toward Luke's picture. "I brought Luke's widow-bride home. I'm only here to see her settled, then I'm gone." His voice softened when he spoke about Cait, so he cleared his throat. "You didn't have to overprice the house so it wouldn't sell. She would have come if you'd asked. She misses him. Hell, even I miss him."

He had to leave. Before he said something sentimental.

"Treat your grandbaby right and you and I won't have any further business."

"Show up here tomorrow at eight o'clock and I'll try you out on the sales floor."

Lucky stopped with one foot out the door. "What makes you think I wouldn't take your business from you brick by brick until it's mine?"

"You're welcome to it." His father convulsed with another coughing fit. "Be here at eight."

CAITLIN STOOD IN THE DOORWAY of the smaller bedroom, her arms resting on top of her stomach when Calhoun walked in well after dark carrying his helmet. The top half of the room had been painted the smoky-blue he'd picked out. The bottom half was papered in narrow-beige-and-wide-blue stripes with the teddy bear border bringing the two halves together.

It was the only unfurnished room in the house.

"You did good, Calhoun."

"Thank you." He put his helmet, his keys and his cell phone on her kitchen counter. "Everybody gone?"

She nodded. "There's chicken left if you're hungry."

"I'll fix myself a plate," he said, moving to the fridge.

"They moved the extra furniture and a few boxes to the shed. John offered to take the U-Haul in, but I didn't know what you wanted to do."

"I'll return it tomorrow." He took off his leather jacket and hung it on the back of a stool, then pulled it up to her kitchen counter and sat. The counter had a panoramic view of the kitchen and room for two more stools. The kitchen had a panoramic view of the rest of the house.

He took a bite of Original Recipe chicken and she added the empty bucket and boxes to the trash bag sitting on the floor next to an unopened box marked Kitchen. There was still plenty to do. Evelyn had offered to come back and help with the unpacking.

"I was thinking I'd install some ceiling fans," he said, putting down the breastbone.

"That'd be nice."

He went over a list of things that needed to be done that she hadn't even thought about. "I know I'm a poor substitute for Luke, Cait." He pushed the paper plate aside. "But I'd like to stick around and see you through this pregnancy. If that's all right with you?"

"I'd like that," she said, wishing he was a hugger. Because she was so happy right now she wanted to hug him.

Calhoun stood and cleared his plate, coming around to her side to throw it out. "I'll be out of your hair once the baby's born."

He went into her bedroom and came back out with his rifle

case. It must have been under her bed because she hadn't seen it earlier.

Her apprehension at having a gun in the house must have shown. "I'm taking it to the gun club tomorrow and keeping it under lock and key." He set the case down on her kitchen table, a dining area carved out between the kitchen and living room, and opened it. "Come here," he said, taking it out of the case.

She took a few hesitant steps toward him, surprised to discover that the rifle came in pieces. He snapped those pieces together with quick, efficient movements. "This rifle is for competition only. It's never been used to kill. I don't want you to be afraid of it," he added, handing it to her.

"It's heavy," she said, feeling the weight of it in both hands.

"That's the new M-40A3, a shoulder-fired weapon. It uses special 7.62 mm rounds. You can change out the 10-power scope for an ANPVS-10 nightscope. Here," he said, coming up behind her and fitting it to her right shoulder. "It's not loaded," he said when she tensed.

Caitlin had a hard time concentrating on what he was trying to show her because of the way he felt snug against her—all those hard muscles against her soft curves—his trigger finger over her trigger finger and his left hand over hers under the barrel.

"Sight down the barrel," he whispered in her right ear, sending chills up and down her spine. "The spotter calls the range and the windage. You dial it in," he said, doing that for their imaginary target. "And then he says, 'Send it.' You pull."

Her body stiffened in response to his words. Her stomach tightened, then relaxed again as a long-forgotten warmth spread upward.

He pulled back.

"Shooting's a perishable skill," he said, packing the case. "I wouldn't want to lose it."

She'd almost lost it! Evidently his "trigger finger" got a lot of practice.

Caitlin wondered where he was going with his gun since he'd said he was taking it to the gun club tomorrow.

Fingering the chain around her neck, she watched through the window above the sink as he crossed the gravel driveway to the shed. He opened the door and pulled the overhead chain to turn the light on. There was a cot, the kind found in an Army/Navy surplus store, made up like a bed. The inside of the shed door had a hand-painted sign hanging from it that read FOB. She knew the military used a lot of acronyms, but what did FOB stand for? She'd never heard it before.

Was he planning on sleeping out there?

He sat on the cot and opened his rifle case again. He took out his weapon with care, then proceeded to clean it with a soft rag. Had that whole thing about him not wanting her to be afraid of *it* been about him not wanting her to be afraid of *him?*

When he saw her standing there, watching him, he got up and closed the swinging door. Because of the crawl space raising the house, the kitchen window was somewhat higher than the high, lattice-covered windows across the front of the shed doors. But not high enough for her to see anything except his head as he sat at the workbench.

She gave up watching and moved away from the window.

After that night drive through the salt lakes in the U-Haul, he probably thought she'd freak out when she saw him cleaning his gun and think he was having another post-traumatic stress moment.

She probably would have.

But she hadn't lied about feeling safe with him.

And she wasn't afraid to have an ex-Marine sniper in her shed cleaning his weapon, as long as it was Calhoun.

ALL THE COMFORTS OF HOME. Lucky had turned off the overhead and continued working by the soft glow of the small black-and-white TV he'd plugged in by the workbench. It had been among his things in storage. He also had a hot plate and minifridge. Along with his camping gear, he was set.

He took out each piece of his weapon and meticulously cleaned it with a soft cloth before putting it back. He'd see Cait through this pregnancy because he owed it to her and to Luke. He'd take care of some family business while he was here because he owed that to himself.

But he'd painted that Forward Operating Base sign on the door as a reminder not to get too comfortable. He was playing a dangerous game with himself, holding Cait the way he had. And make no mistake about it, it had been just an excuse to hold her. Her and the baby. In his arms.

It's where they belonged. Yet there was nothing about him that deserved it. Cait had been Luke's wife. And if Lucky was ever going to really forgive himself for his past, he'd have to honor that.

He took out his nightscope and blew on the lens, not that he'd find a speck of dust, then rubbed it with a clean cloth on both ends. He glanced through the crosshairs and wiped it down again.

The lights were off in the house.

He aimed his nightscope in that direction. Through the

kitchen window he could see the faucet and sink, unpacked boxes. And he had an unobstructed view of Cait lying on the couch in front of the TV.

His heart pounded.

He took deep, even breaths until he and the blood thrumming through his veins were one. A sniper observed his world from a distance. He wasn't part of it.

And if he needed a reminder of that, he had only to focus on the wedding DVD Cait was watching. After several minutes of observing her from a distance he put his scope away.

The only person he was a danger to was himself.

"SO, YOU SHOWED UP," BIG LUKE said the following morning at eight o'clock when Lucky marched across the showroom floor of Calhoun Cycles.

Because he had something to prove.

Big Luke looked him up and down, in his jeans and leather jacket. "The job doesn't require a shirt and tie, but we do have a dress code." Lucky had seen the polo shirts worn by the sales staff with the Calhoun Cycles logo. He didn't want one.

"I'm not here to sell your bikes."

Big Luke knew him well enough to know what he did want. "No son of mine is working in the back."

"Those are my conditions. And consider this temporary."

He didn't need this job. He needed to live up to the man he'd become as a Marine, not the boy who'd ran away from here. And when he walked away this time, and he would walk away again, it would be on his terms.

"You never had a problem with the grease under my nails

before," Lucky said. He'd worked in his father's garage as unpaid help as a teen, both of them pretending he wasn't back there building his bikes, learning the business, soaking it all in.

Luke had been the face of their father's business in his fancy motocross gear. But of Big Luke's three sons, only Lucky had the same fire and passion in his gut for motorcycles.

Lucky maybe could have turned his racing career into something if it hadn't been all about getting even with Luke.

If he hadn't run away.

Without another word, Big Luke changed direction and headed to the four bays out back. These garages were newer, cleaner, but his father had retained the same parts-and-service manager.

"Hey, if it isn't my old sidekick," greeted an older Jose, who was slower to his feet as he pushed up from a crouch next to a broken-down bike. "You coming back to work with us, Junior?"

It had been a long time since anyone called him anything other than Lucky.

CALHOUN CYCLES WAS farther along Broadway than Caitlin had thought and she was glad she hadn't decided to walk.

After a week of volunteering, she'd taken time off to unpack, and now she needed a break from unpacking.

She entered a large showroom with several attentive employees.

"I'm here to see Big Luke. Can you tell him it's his daughter-in-law, Caitlin?" She followed the salesman past row upon row of motorcycles until she got sidetracked by the showcase tribute to Luke.

It would have been nice if it wasn't so tacky.

Big Luke's office was in sight of the showroom, and she watched through the glass as the salesman told Big Luke she was here. Big Luke looked up, then headed her way.

"Cait," he greeted her with that trademark big smile she'd seen on TV. "How's my grandbaby? Kickin' up a fuss, I bet."

"You're exactly right about that." This Calhoun was already shooting hoops.

"Come on in." Big Luke closed his office door behind them. "Can I get you anything? Coffee, water?"

She accepted a bottle of water. "Actually, I came to thank you again for the house and to ask a big favor."

"Anything. Sit down," he urged when she remained standing. "How much do you need?" he asked, getting out his checkbook.

"No," Caitlin said, embarrassed, "this isn't about money."

"Nonsense, you just reminded me I haven't given you a housewarming gift." He ripped out the check and handed it to her. She looked at the amount in her hand, a thousand dollars, and immediately thought of Calhoun's scholarship fund for Peanut.

Peanut needed her to pick out a new name.

One that wouldn't hurt Calhoun every time he heard it.

"This is too generous. And not why I'm here… It's about your commercial. And Little Luke's uniform on display…" She stated her misgivings as she'd rehearsed them. He nodded throughout but didn't say a word. When she finished she thanked him for his time and got up to leave.

Caitlin hesitated in the doorway.

"Junior's around back," he said, without her having to ask.

CAITLIN FOLLOWED BIG LUKE'S directions to a humming four-bay garage. Calhoun spotted her first and met her halfway.

"Everything okay?" His eyes went immediately to her stomach as he wiped his greasy hands on a rag.

"I just wanted to see where you worked," she said. "And I thought maybe you'd let me buy you lunch."

"How about I buy you lunch?"

"Okay." She didn't argue. He was the one with the paying job. She just volunteered. She still had money in the bank and Luke's pension. And her cost of living was now half what it had been. But she needed to scrimp if she was going to take any time with the baby before looking for work.

They hadn't seen much of each other these past two weeks. He left early and came back late. Then, after checking in with her, he did some work around the house or yard, then went out to the shed for the night.

"Let me get cleaned up," he said. When he came back, they walked without talking until they placed their lunch order at the closest Subway sandwich counter.

"So you've been busy," she said outside, after they'd gotten their food. Busy keeping his distance. And she didn't know how to tell him she missed spending time with him. She wondered how this restaurant compared to the Subway at Camp Victory and if Calhoun missed any part of being a Marine.

Did he miss his uniform?

Marines had a handsome dress uniform, and after her talk with Big Luke earlier she had uniforms on the brain. The very first thing she'd noticed about Luke had been his dress whites. Silly, but it was enough to get her to take a second look and to say yes when he'd asked her out on that first date.

Big Luke had mentioned Little Luke's joining the Naval Academy with the intention of becoming a Marine officer. But he'd become a Naval officer instead.

That had been years before she'd met him. And another piece of trivia she hadn't known about her husband. But today she wasn't going to feel sad about that.

Headed back to the garage, Calhoun steered her in the direction of a picnic table under a shade tree.

There was a smokeless ashtray at either end. Was this where all the smokers hung out on their breaks? She hadn't seen Calhoun light up again. And he didn't smell like tobacco. But he still carried around that pack of cigarettes he'd bought on their road trip.

Or was that another pack of cigarettes?

She hoped not.

"So I found an ob/gyn. Did you want to come?" she asked him.

"Where?" He stood there, looking confused.

"To my seventh-month ob/gyn appointment in two weeks?"

She'd be seven months plus one week pregnant to be exact, but that was the earliest she could be squeezed in.

He looked like a man given the choice between tar pits and quicksand.

"You'd hear the baby's heartbeat."

OVER THE COURSE OF THE NEXT two weeks, Caitlin volunteered at the VA Hospital just enough to keep busy. In California she'd taken the California Pharmacy Jurisprudence Exam,

CPJE. In Colorado she had to take the Multi-State Pharmacy Jurisprudence Exam, MPJE. She also had to provide documentation of her degree and continuing education hours to apply for her license. And she discovered that establishing herself in a new state with a new doctor in her seventh month was a bit unnerving. The next appointment in three weeks would be her eighth month, then biweekly and weekly.

She was in the home stretch.

The last trimester.

Calhoun was waiting for her in the tastefully decorated waiting room, looking uncomfortable in his casual work clothes, when she walked in carrying a bottle of water. But no more uncomfortable than she was having to drink and hold what felt like a gallon of water before her ultrasound.

She'd come directly from her patients on the amputee floor and wore yellow scrubs today.

"Busy place," he commented once she was seated beside him.

"Sign of a good ob/gyn." She'd met Doctor Jennifer Buhr at the VA Hospital. Though the woman was not a military doctor, she did contract with the military and was established with several other area hospitals, including the one Caitlin had chosen right next door to the VA. Equally important, she accepted Caitlin's insurance.

"Caitlin?" The nurse called them to the inner sanctum.

Calhoun hesitated and Cait had to haul him in with her.

"Go ahead and step on the scale, please," the nurse said.

Cait slipped out of her shoes first. And sighed. She was up twenty pounds from that fateful first visit to the fertility specialist. And she was only going to get fatter. Calhoun cocked an eyebrow when he saw her weight, and she wanted to hit him.

The nurse took her blood pressure next.

"I really need to pee," Caitlin said.

"Just enough to relieve yourself. Your bladder needs to be full for the ultrasound." The nurse handed her a specimen cup. "May as well get a sample while you're at it."

Calhoun looked as if he wanted to run.

Neither of them had brought up CryoBank since the day she'd found out there would be no more Calhoun babies for her. Luke's. Or Calhoun's.

When Caitlin was finished, the nurse showed them to a room. Calhoun camped out in a corner while Caitlin sat on the table. Leaning back, she scratched at her baby bump and looked over her shoulder at him. "It itches all over."

The doctor knocked, then entered, reading Cait's chart before closing it to greet them. She was young. Maybe just out of med school.

"Cait, it's good to see you again. Hi—" she held out her hand to Calhoun "—I'm Dr. Jennifer Buhr. And you must be Cait's donor/brother-in-law." They shook and maybe held hands a little too long as far as Caitlin was concerned.

"We're just going to get a few measurements today," she explained, to put him at ease. "No wallflowers allowed in this room." She drew Calhoun in close with her words and with her smile. "Go ahead and lie back, Cait." Dr. Buhr helped her.

"So you were a Marine?" she asked Calhoun. "Where were you stationed?"

"Camp Pendleton. San Diego, California."

"I don't know, Cait," the doctor teased while exposing Cait's stomach. "Seems to me like your brother-in-law is the strong, silent type. See any action?" she asked him.

"He's just back from Iraq," Cait said, feeling irritated that she wasn't the one the doctor was interested in.

The doctor took out her tape measure and took Cait's measurements. She gave Cait her complete attention for the next several minutes. Hanging the tape measure around her neck, she put her hands it the pockets of her white lab coat.

"Have you heard the baby's heartbeat yet?" she asked Calhoun. "You're in for a real treat."

CHAPTER TEN

"I CAN'T BELIEVE MY OB/GYN was flirting with my brother-in-law over my bare belly!" Caitlin said as soon as they stepped outside the doctor's office. "But what I really can't believe is that she asked you out on a date and you accepted!"

"Cait," he said with more patience than she deserved, "she asked you if it would be all right first. Then I asked you."

"You put me on the spot. You're not supposed to ask in front of her. What could I say?"

"No."

"Ha!" She stormed off ahead of him.

It took him only two strides to catch up. "So I take it you're not okay with this?" He unclipped his cell phone.

"You can't call off the date! Do you have any idea what this means? If things end badly between the two of you I'm going to have to find a new ob/gyn in my *eighth* month."

"You know, Cait, it isn't always about you." He headed toward the parking garage.

It took her a lot longer than two strides to catch up to him. "What do you mean it isn't about me?"

He exhaled as he turned to her under the covered parking. "It's been a really long time for me. She's an attractive woman. I'd like to go out on a date. And I didn't think I needed your permission to do that."

He meant sex. "Of course you don't."

"Do you need a ride?" he offered. "I have one of the company cars."

"No," she said, about to let him go. "Oh, the nurse handed me this on the way out." She dug the flyer about Lamaze classes out of her purse. "Would Monday/Wednesday or Tuesday/Thursday nights work better for you?" She looked at him expectantly.

"Is that really brother-in-law duty?" he asked. "Don't you think you should be asking Nora Jean? If she can't swing it I'm sure Dottie would be more than happy to fill in." He made it worse by making up an excuse. "I'm really busy at the shop. I have this bike I'm working on—"

"No," she said, embarrassed and disappointed, "you're right. I shouldn't have asked you."

"I'll see you after work."

And he'd be seeing her doctor this weekend.

"See you after work," she repeated. But she didn't go back to volunteering that afternoon. She got out her cell phone and called Nora Jean.

THEY WERE PRICING BABY furniture at Babies R Us. "Do you like this one?" her mother-in-law asked, turning over the price tag.

"Too expensive."

Nora Jean sighed and moved on. Her mother-in-law had been twenty when she had Luke. She was in her late forties. Fit. And well-groomed. Her medium-length, light brown hair had been highlighted by a professional colorist, reminding Caitlin she needed to get that stylist's number.

"Did I tell you Big Luke has agreed to shoot a new commercial?" Nora Jean asked. "He called and told me last week. I knew if I went in there with both guns blazing he'd see it my way."

"That's nice," Cait agreed, hoping her talk with Big Luke had helped, too.

You know, Cait, it isn't always about you.

She'd needed that reality check from Calhoun.

"Is *he* still sleeping out in your shed?" Her mother-in-law raised her eyebrow. "Luke would not approve, Caitlin."

Caitlin didn't like how Nora Jean loved to complain about Calhoun. Caitlin thought she wanted that today, too. But now that Nora Jean was being true to form Caitlin realized she didn't want to gripe about him.

He'd been very good to her, and if he wanted to date, well, he was a big boy. "He's welcome to stay as long as he'd like."

It's just that she kept associating the word *date* with the word *sex,* and she couldn't shake the image of him with his arms wrapped around her attractive ob/gyn. His big hands splayed across the other woman's flat stomach and going lower with that trigger finger.

"I mean, does it have to be my ob/gyn?"

"What?" Nora Jean looked at her, perplexed. "Oh, you can always find a nurse midwife if you don't want to deliver with an ob/gyn. As I was saying," Nora Jean continued, "we'd like to throw you a baby shower."

"I don't really know anybody here—"

"We thought your new place would be neutral ground."

"Who's *we?*"

"Dottie, Evelyn and I. That makes the three of us, some of your coworkers at the hospital… Calhoun Cycles has a couple of female employees. And if we're going to do that then we'd have to invite Maddie. But I think we could throw you a nice shower."

They'd moved out of furniture and over to clothes.

"I don't know.…" A baby T-shirt caught her eye.

"Oh, Caitlin, why do you have to be so difficult? With Luke gone, this is my first and only grandbaby. Do it for me?"

"Okay," Caitlin relented. *For Luke.*

"You wait right here. I'm going to go get you registered." Nora Jean left her alone to look at the little boys' clothes.

Caitlin kept coming back round to that T-shirt.

Gray with blue block lettering. Little Guy.

And the matching daddy T-shirt. Big Guy.

When Nora Jean came back the only thing Caitlin really wanted wasn't added to her registry.

LUCKY WAS STANDING ON A LADDER, hooking up a ceiling fan in Cait's bedroom when she came home. "Where've you been?" he asked, trying not to sound overbearing.

"Baby shopping," she said, staring up at the new ceiling fan. "That looks nice."

She didn't walk in with any shopping bags. "You want to flip the switch?" He'd replaced the single switch with a double, one of them a three-way that controlled the speed. "Hit it again."

"How'd you do that?" she asked as she cycled through the different speeds.

"And there's a remote on the bed," he said, pointing.

"Just what I need, another remote."

"Do you want me to set everything up for you on a universal remote?" he asked, climbing down.

"Are you kidding? That's way too complicated for me."

"Then building a new garage is the next project. You'll want someplace to put your car come winter. I'm trying to get you a Calhoun Cycles company car so you don't have to keep racking up mileage on that Mustang of yours." He kept talking and waiting for her to notice the furniture in the corner. Finally, he just cocked his head toward the window.

"You brought in a chair and an ottoman," she said, walking over and putting her feet up.

Nothing fancy. Just something he'd had in storage that they'd brought with them. The deep maroon leather went with her neutral—pink—color scheme.

"I bet I have a reading lamp and a small table out in the shed to turn this into a reading nook," Cait said.

She didn't get up right away. Her hand went to her stomach. "Or I could nurse the baby here," she said, guessing his intent. She sat there daydreaming for a moment and when she turned to the left she noticed the picture at her eye level. "Is that the Point Loma lighthouse?" she asked with wonder, looking at it more closely. "That's the exact view from the window in my old apartment. How did you get that, Calhoun?"

With the help of Bruce and Mrs. Pèna.

"That's my secret," he said.

Bruce had downloaded the picture on his cell phone, and Lucky had taken it to Kinko's for the reproduction and then had it framed.

"Thank you," she said, pushing up from the chair belly-first. He noticed she was having more trouble getting in and out of chairs these days. Her hand went to the small of her back. And her stomach was just there, between them, inviting his touch. While he was thinking about it, she reached up to brush his hair. "You're still getting a weekly haircut, I see."

Their bodies were so close he didn't have to touch her to feel Peanut's movement. But all he could concentrate on was her fingertips at his temple. And her parted lips.

She leaned in and at the last second veered toward his cheek. "That was really sweet what you did," she said in a voice as soft as her kiss.

The doorbell rang, surprising them both.

Nobody ever rang the front doorbell.

"I'll get it," she said.

When he came out of the bedroom carrying the ladder, she was staring at the door. The doorbell rang a second time. "You need to get it," she said, backing away.

On full alert, he propped the ladder against the wall. Something had terrified her.

"It's an official military car," she said as he reached her. "A Marine in full-dress uniform." She clutched at his forearm. "Do you think something's happened to Bruce?"

The doorbell rang a third time.

Cait had a lot of anniversaries coming up in the next few weeks and months. What would have been her first wedding anniversary. The anniversary of Luke's deployment. The anniversary of Luke's death.

He realized that when the doorbell had rung, her first thought had gone to the official notification of her husband's death. His thoughts were less ominous. He'd just spoken with

Bruce today. The Marine Corps didn't know he was here. So unless a buddy had tracked him down…

He opened the door to find a young private standing there. He didn't know Private Hobbs, but his name tag and car identified him as a Marine recruiter.

This ought to be good.

"Can I help you?" he asked in his best Sergeant Stryker tone.

"I have a delivery for a Master Sergeant Luke Calhoun Jr. from a Master Sergeant Hobbs."

"He's one of the patients on my ward," Cait explained.

"Yes, ma'am." The young Marine tipped his cap. "My grandfather asked me to deliver this box to this address. To a Master Sergeant—"

"Calhoun." She elbowed him in the ribs. "That's you."

The *master sergeant* accepted the box grudgingly while the young private beat a hasty retreat.

The box was whining. And the weight shifted.

There were two words written across the top.

Teufel Hunden.

Devil dog.

"You've got to be kidding" was all Lucky could say.

"Aren't Marines 'devil dogs'?" she asked. "Wouldn't proper German for Devil Dogs be *Teufelshunde?*"

"Not if you ask a Marine."

"What are you afraid of, Calhoun? Open the box."

He set it down on the nearby coffee table. "Have at it."

Cait lifted the lid. "Oh, isn't he precious?"

"He looks damn ugly to me." He sized up the English bulldog puppy. "And he's going to get even uglier."

"Come here, baby," she said to the puppy.

"BABY PRACTICE," BRUCE SAID over the long-distance call.

"What?" Lucky was stretched out on his rack in the FOB with his ear to his cell phone and the "baby" asleep on his chest. He petted the dog absently.

"Puppies are baby practice. She's giving you baby practice."

"Cait didn't give me the mutt. A friend of hers did."

"A close friend? Someone she confides in?"

"A crotchety old master sergeant on the hospital ward where she volunteers, from what I understand."

"Hmm," Bruce said thoughtfully. "Next thing you know you'll be going to birthing and breast-feeding classes."

"They have classes for breast-feeding?"

He was in way the hell over his head.

Hearing his baby's heartbeat today, that was a big deal. Lamaze classes would have been a bigger deal. He couldn't be there for her, for the birth, then just walk away from his son after delivery.

He couldn't be this guy, Uncle Lucky.

"Her ob asked me out on a date."

"You're dating Cait's doctor?"

"We haven't even had a first date yet." But at least with Jennifer he didn't have to pretend to be anything other than what he was. The brother-in-law/donor/very confused father-to-be.

"Anyway, she says I have to name it."

"What?"

"Cait says I have to name the mutt."

"So, what are you going to name it?" Bruce asked.

"That's why I called you."

"Just pick a name. Something tough so you don't feel stupid when you have to say it."

The puppy began to stir. "Gotta go tinkle," Lucky said, hanging up to the sound of his brother's laughter.

After the dog finished his business, Lucky picked it up and carried it into the kitchen.

When Cait looked up, "Sergeant Stryker" was all he said.

THE NIGHT OF HIS BIG DATE arrived. They were meeting at LoDo's for drinks. If drinks went well they'd progress to dinner. At least that's how he thought this worked. There'd be the phone call from the friend. And she'd either tell him she had an emergency and had to leave, or she'd tell her friend things were going well and stay.

An awful lot riding on one drink.

But if that first date went well, then he'd be obligated to call her for a second. A second might lead to a third. And before he knew it they'd be dating. That's what he wanted, wasn't it?

Somebody who was actually available to date him.

She was at the bar when he walked in. Her dress was black, and he almost laughed at the irony when all he could think about was Cait with nothing to wear. Cait calling herself fat. Cait so swollen from carrying his child she couldn't get her wedding rings back on her finger.

Cait, who couldn't get out of a chair, while the graceful doctor uncrossed her long legs and headed toward him.

He found them a table and ordered their drinks. The place was crowded and loud, and he didn't know how any first-date drinks progressed to dinner here.

But he leaned in close enough to listen and did his best to

hold up his end of the conversation. When the call came he was almost disappointed, knowing he had this whole first-date thing figured out. Of course, that's what happened after thirty-two years of being single.

He got out his own cell phone while he waited, hoping for a moment that her call was a real emergency. After all, the doctor delivered babies.

He had no new messages.

But he cursed under his breath when he saw the date. How could he be so stupid?

"A friend checking in," she admitted when she hung up. And he liked her all the more for her honesty.

He was in the clear. That was his opportunity to ask her to dinner. "Jennifer," he said, "I have go. I'm sorry. I just realized it's Cait and Luke's first anniversary. I don't think she should be alone tonight."

"Of course not," she agreed with a measure of real concern in her voice. "Did you need me to come with you?" she asked as he stood.

"No," he said. "Just promise me Cait won't have to look for a new ob/gyn because of my stupidity."

LUCKY KNEW EVEN BEFORE HE walked in the door where he'd find her. On the couch, in that ratty T-shirt of Luke's, watching her wedding DVD.

Wedding-themed wrapping paper was strewn from one end of the house to the other. She sat on the couch amid boxes and bags and her opened wedding gifts. Petting his Devil Dog.

She looked up when he walked in and choked back a sob.

Her lower lip trembled.

Tears streamed down her face.

She pushed belly-up from the couch. He was across the room in two strides to help her.

"What about your date?"

"Emergency," he said.

She sniffed. "I hate to tell you this, Calhoun. But the girl-friend call is the oldest trick in the book."

His focus narrowed to her mouth. "My emergency."

Her lips parted. "What—"

"This," he said against her lips, tasting the salt of her tears. That first tentative touch of their lips was so sweet she melted into him. He wrapped her in his arms and she wound hers around his neck.

He'd thought about nothing else but her the entire ride home. How wrong it was to want her. And he wondered now how anything so wrong could feel so right.

He freed her falling hair from the lose rubber band and tangled his hand in it. He deepened their kiss with a sense of urgency even he didn't know he was feeling.

His breath became hot. And labored.

The baby moved and he adjusted his position as he adjusted to the idea of it. He cupped her full breast through the thin material of Luke's worn T-shirt, his thumb finding the hardened peak of her nipple.

He untangled himself from her hair as he became greedy for her soft flesh. He pulled at the hem of her shirt as she hurried to unbutton his.

The blood pumped south of his brain as his hands memorized her every curve. He pushed her panties down to dip his fingers in hidden places.

She threw her head back and called out his name.

"Oh, Luke."

"CAIT!" CALHOUN POUNDED ON THE bathroom door. "Cait, please come out of there."

She tried to cry silently, tried to kill the pain. But her sobs kept breaking through. *Oh, Luke.*

"I want to be alone right now."

"Cait, we need to talk about this."

"I don't want to talk."

"Just let me in so I can see you're all right." It sounded like a reasonable request. But she didn't move, not even to unlock the door.

She sat on the edge of the tub, rocking.

But as soon as he tested the other knob, she realized she'd forgotten to lock both doors. He opened the other one with an audible sigh of relief.

Putting the toilet lid down, he sat. "Cait—"

She recoiled from his touch.

This was wrong. This was so wrong.

She loved Luke.

She wanted Calhoun.

"I just wanted to have his baby," she sobbed. "I never asked for this."

"I know, I know." He pulled her into his lap and she didn't protest. He rocked her until her sobs subsided. And she clung to him until she fell asleep.

Night after night Lucky lay on his rack in the FOB, staring at the ceiling, telling himself he wasn't going to run this time. Things had changed between him and Cait.

There was a tension they didn't talk about. It sucked the air right out of the room whenever they shared the same space, making it hard to breathe.

Even that was preferable to the emptiness he felt when he was alone.

Stroking Sergeant Stryker, he listened to the rumble of thunder in the distance. Life was simpler when your first order of business was your day-to-day survival. If only he could put this in the context of a military operation, he could plan his next course of action.

"You've had your revenge," he said. "She loves you. She doesn't want me."

Rain followed the thunder. Then the first drops found the holes in the roof, hitting the pots he'd strategically placed around the room.

He'd hung a tarp and moved his rack to the driest spot in the shed. He'd covered the important pieces of furniture in plastic. Until he could get the new garage built he should pick up one of those portable car ports for Cait's Mustang. Tomorrow he'd go do that and get a tarp big enough to cover the whole roof and check out the roof of the house.

He thought of Cait, warm and dry inside.

He thought of Cait, wet to his touch.

He got hard just thinking about it. He moved Stryker off his chest and put the puppy in his own bed on a folded blanket underneath the rack.

He lay with his forearm shading his eyes from the flashes

of lightning, and must have fallen asleep. He opened them again at the sound of a creak.

His first clue that Cait had come into the shed.

The second was her staring down at him from the foot of his bed. She was damp and shivering, but not from the cold. It was late spring and the temperature was warm outside.

He watched as a single drop of rain landed on her T-shirt right above her nipple to join with other drops to create a sheer view of that hardened peak.

"Say something," she breathed.

"What do you want me to say?"

He didn't move. She did, crawling over him until they were face-to-face. Her belly brushed his stomach. Her hair, his face. He felt the press of her knees to his hips where she straddled him, but other than that they weren't touching. Yet he felt every inch of her in the electricity passing between them.

She dipped her head to kiss him, but he didn't meet her halfway and she stopped, uncertain. "I'm tired of fighting it," she whispered. "Kiss me, Calhoun."

He made it long and slow this time. Afraid she'd slip though his fingers if he dared reach for her.

She sat back.

He saw confusion in her eyes.

"What's wrong?" She bit down on her bottom lip.

"Nothing's wrong." He dropped his legs over the sides of his rack and sat up underneath her. "You just need to let me know if you're just testing the waters. Because in about a minute I'm going to be inside you. And I'm not going to stop, even if you're screaming his name."

He fit her to the length of him so she could feel his heat as his words sank in. He watched her breasts rise and fall on a shuddered breath.

"I want you, Calhoun," she breathed.

He stood, taking her with him. She clung to his shoulders and he hitched her legs up around his waist. "That cot only holds three hundred pounds," he said, "and it's hanging over the puppy's bed. If you still want me in the time it takes me to carry you across this driveway to your bed…then heaven help us both, you can have me."

"SAY IT AGAIN," HE SAID, laying her on her bed. He held his body over hers and teased her, with his mouth so close to her lips they should have been kissing.

Caitlin inched up to reach him. He pulled back.

"Say it," he commanded, pulling his shirt off over his head.

She traced every inch of blue-green ink radiating from the Celtic cross at his collarbone.

First with her eyes. Then with her lips.

"I want you, Calhoun."

His body—with or without tattoos—was a work of art. His muscles were honed from the daily discipline and exercise required to be a Marine. And a routine he'd continued long after he'd made it.

He was solid. And he was a real man.

His mouth became more demanding with each successive kiss. It frightened her that she could meet that demand with a passion she thought had died with Luke.

Calhoun wasn't her Luke. And she didn't want him to be anyone other than who he was.

Was that wrong? Was she thinking clearly?

She didn't know. And at this moment she didn't care.

All she wanted was to stop the ache that had kept her awake for too many nights.

Clothes became an obstacle that had to be removed. Once they were removed there was a bigger obstacle in the form of her bulging belly, but not one that couldn't be overcome.

She straddled him and he eased himself into her body, eased the ache.

She had an awkward rhythm and he helped her into that, too.

She threw her head back and closed her eyes until he made her look at him. "Say it again."

"I want you, Calhoun," Caitlin said over and over again until she was completely sated.

When he wrapped her in that arm with the intricate tribal design, she felt protected.

CHAPTER ELEVEN

"WHERE DO YOU THINK YOU'RE going?" Cait hauled him back into bed and snuggled up against his bare backside.

"You're insatiable," Lucky said, rolling toward her.

"Hmm…I'm hormonal." She closed her eyes and a smile curved her lips.

"I'm just going for my run." He may fall asleep in her bed every night, but that didn't mean he felt he belonged there. He stole out of her bed at the crack of dawn just to try to put it all in perspective.

He cleared his throat to broach a subject he'd been trying to get her to talk about ever since that first night they'd made love. "I think we should have talked about this before becoming lovers, Cait."

"Lovers," she said, propping herself up on her elbow and giving him her full attention. "Is that what we are? Don't sweat it, Calhoun. I know this is just a fling. Nora Jean will be here all the time after the baby's born. My father's coming for a visit. I won't even be able to have sex for six weeks. I'm sure I won't feel like it, anyway, because I'll be busy with the baby. So you can leave with a clear conscience anytime you want. Just not this morning," she said.

What about a contingency plan for his staying?

Looking at her, he didn't ask.

They never talked about future plans because they didn't have any. There'd be no room in her life for him, not even as a lover, after the baby.

He was still Luke's brother, the baby's Uncle Lucky—the guy who'd breeze in on birthdays and Christmases.

The guy who was falling in love with his sister-in-law, the mother of his child, and didn't know what the hell to do about it.

THE DISPLAY CASE CAITLIN HAD asked Big Luke to order on her first visit to Calhoun Cycles had arrived. She had plenty of time to put it together before the commercial shoot tomorrow. So when Maddie, Big Luke's current wife, tempted her with a mother-to-be makeover, Caitlin accepted.

Caitlin was relaxing with a fruit-juice spritzer in the lounge. The log cabin–like atmosphere was anything but rustic and provided the perfect mountain view from the tall windows throughout the five-star resort.

Maddie sat down and showed Cait the new ring she'd purchased to show off her manicure. "He'll be mad when he gets the bill," she was saying about her credit card spending. "But what the hell, he's got the money and he can't take it with him, right?"

It wasn't that Caitlin disliked Maddie, but she'd had enough already.

She reached into her own shopping bag and pulled out the matching T-shirts to show Maddie.

Big Guy. Little Guy.

The purchase had been a guilty indulgence. She didn't

even know if she'd ever give it to him. Only that they'd created an impossible situation for themselves, made all the more difficult by becoming lovers.

The truth would hurt too many people. And the deception… It had never felt like a deception until now. The sperm bank mix-up wasn't his fault. And she wasn't going to tie him down because of it.

"Isn't that cute," Maddie said. "I want a baby," she whined. "And not just because of the prenup, either. But of course, the chemo and radiation fried his sperm."

"Big Luke has cancer?"

"He had a lung removed last year. He's in remission now, but who knows how long he has. The doctor told him to give up smoking, and he didn't. I'd give up smoking if I were pregnant," Maddie said in her rather roundabout logic. "And if I were pregnant Big Luke would have to give up smoking, too."

Cait was still trying to digest the news of Big Luke's remission from lung cancer. She knew people didn't have to smoke to get the disease. But it seemed as if a life-threatening illness should have been enough to make both Big Luke and Maddie quit smoking. And if not, she doubted either of them would quit for a baby.

"Maddie, give up smoking first."

LATER THAT AFTERNOON CAITLIN stopped by the VA hospital and checked in on her favorite patient.

"Guess you really are an apothecary," he said when she showed off her license to Master Sergeant Hobbs. His voice lacked his usual boom. Caitlin adjusted his pillows without a single complaint out of him.

She'd read his charts. His stump wasn't healing. His body wasn't fighting off the infection. He was losing his battle with diabetes.

"Stryker won't leave his side," she said.

"He's taken a real shine to him, then?"

"They've taken a real shine to each other." She smiled sadly. Would he take Stryker with him when he left? Or would he leave Stryker with her?

She showed Master Sergeant Hobbs the T-shirts she'd purchased.

"I want to hear more about that new house of yours."

"You mean I haven't bored you with the details?"

"So, you let him pick out the color to the nursery. What color did he pick?" he asked, laying his head back against the pillow and closing his eyes.

"Blue."

BLUE FLAMES, ON BLUE. Lucky crouched to admire the custom paint job on the first bike crafted to his own custom design. He'd worked many hours to get this machine done. It didn't hurt that he had an entire staff and everything he needed at his disposal.

Big Luke had been very generous.

Making up for lost time?

Guilty conscience?

It didn't matter. The past was history.

"What are you going to name it?" Jose asked as he free-handed the finishing touches to the flames with a fine paintbrush. Jose was a master of detail artistry.

Cait was the first name that came to mind. But a street bike needed a biker name. Something tough.

"Stryker," he said.

Jose chose his angle carefully and painted it on.

For the most part Big Luke left Lucky alone to run their new customization service. He briefed the old man on those things he thought Big Luke should know about and didn't bother him with the day-to-day operations.

Speak of the devil. Lucky pushed to his feet as Big Luke headed his way.

He stopped to look at the bike.

"Nice job," he said, giving it his patent understated approval. "Let's use it in the commercial tomorrow."

CAITLIN SPENT THE FOLLOWING morning at Calhoun Cycles, putting together her display. Her heart filled with pride for Luke.

The case was backed against a wall, where it could be considered inconspicuous, but where customers might also wander over and take a look.

The male bust filled out the uniform nicely.

These ribbons and medals were actually ones he'd received, including his posthumous Purple Heart.

She'd stopped by the Army/Navy surplus for accessories, putting the hat and gloves at just the right angle.

And she'd included a picture of their wedding and of his funeral. And a sampling of their letters.

A brass plate on the woodblock stated his name and rank on one line, Lieutenant Luke Calhoun, and his date of birth to date of death on the next. Below that, his date of service.

Big Luke came out of his office to admire her handiwork. "Here," he said. "You asked about Luke's motocross days. I dug these up for you." He handed her a stack of videotapes. "Old family movies of Luke I haven't had transferred to DVD yet."

"Thank you. I can do that for you," she said, accepting the tapes.

He nodded toward the display case. "That's going to look real nice for the commercial, Cait."

"Remember, nothing too overt. You're going to stand right here—" she indicated the tape on the floor beside Luke's display case "—and say…"

"CALHOUN CYCLES, A TRADITION of proud service."

"Cut!" the director yelled. "That's a keeper, Mr. Big. Now the one with Junior and the puppy in the shot."

"On your marks."

They moved into place, standing side-by-side with Lucky holding the puppy.

"And mark."

"Scene Two. Take One."

"Calhoun Cycles, a tradition of proud service," they said in unison half a dozen times. Then Lucky had to repeat that another half-dozen while crouching to pet Sergeant Stryker. Then they moved the whole thing outside for a wide-angle shot of all the Calhoun Cycles' employees in the parking lot, the service staff lined up behind Lucky and the sales staff lined up behind his father.

Maddie, of course, as his father's secretary and wife, was in the picture. And when the director mistook Cait for Lucky's pregnant wife as she was standing on the sidelines, he pulled her and the puppy in, too.

According to the director, pregnant women and puppies tugged at the heartstrings.

He didn't have to tell Lucky that.

LUCKY RUSHED HOME WITH STRYKER at the end of another long day to find Cait in bed with a bag of potato chips. She was wearing Luke's T-shirt as she lay surrounded by videotapes. Homemade movies from the look of it.

"Everything all right?" he asked, putting the puppy down on the bed.

"Uh-huh," she answered without looking at him.

She put another chip in her mouth, and he glanced at the motocross race on the screen. More old tapes of Luke? No wonder she looked as if she'd been crying.

"Wait." She stopped him as he turned to leave.

She picked up the remote and aimed it at the TV. "I think this is the part where you break his collarbone." She turned the volume way up.

He didn't have to see the screen to know which race that was. She looked at him, and he saw the accusation in her expression.

She reached behind her for a pillow and threw it at him. He knocked it to the floor. She threw the remote and hit him in the chest. It fell and the batteries rolled out, across the floor.

"I'm not that kid anymore, Cait" was all he said in his own defense. He slept in the FOB that night with Stryker.

ON THE EVENING OF HER BABY shower, Caitlin had taken half a day just to get out of bed. Her back ached and it upset her to realize just how deep Calhoun's hatred for her husband ran.

That one race wasn't the only evidence. There were many instances of his aggression toward Luke caught on tape.

Nora Jean arrived early to decorate. Evelyn and Dottie arrived after work with the cake. Calhoun was nowhere to be found. Cait hadn't seen him since she'd thrown the remote.

When the guests arrived, all she could think was who were these people—these strangers showering her baby with gifts? She must have smiled her way through it. She just didn't remember.

When it was over, Dottie cleared her living room while Evelyn helped Caitlin clean up in the kitchen and Nora Jean took inventory.

"Who in the world gave you this?" She came out of the nursery with a Babies R Us bag. She plucked the Big Guy T-shirt from the bag and held it up. "How inappropriate," she said, tossing it aside.

Then she went into the living room for more stuff to haul into the nursery.

Evelyn glanced at Caitlin. "Cait, you look exhausted," Evelyn said in a voice meant to carry into the living room. Then Evelyn had a quiet word with Nora Jean and Dottie and the other two women left.

When Evelyn came back into the kitchen she plucked the T-shirt off the floor, where it had dropped. "You did a pretty good job of faking it tonight," Evelyn said, folding the Big Guy T-shirt and putting it back in the bag with Little Guy. "I don't think anyone knew your heart was broken. What'd he do?"

"I wish I had a mother like you." Cait threw her arms around Evelyn's neck. "Why does he hate Luke so much, Evelyn?"

Evelyn took a step back and sat down, patting the stool beside her. "Luke was seven when he stopped going by 'Junior.'"

That got Cait's attention. She sat down. His mother never used Calhoun's given name. And she was talking about Calhoun—Cait could tell by the way the woman's voice had taken on a note of nostalgia.

"We were in the grocery store when we bumped into Nora Jean. Bruce and Little Luke must have been about three. Bruce was in the cart, but Luke was too big. And Little Luke was running all over the aisle.

"Nora Jean and I had never been on the best of terms," she continued. "I must have said something about getting her child under control. Anyway, Big Luke boomed from the end of the aisle, '*Luke, come here.*' When their father spoke like that the boys listened."

While Caitlin fidgeted, Evelyn continued. "Luke thought his father was speaking to him. He took a couple steps in that direction. Big Luke picked up Little Luke and left…. The boys knew each other from visitation, of course. But his father had a new wife and a new family, and I think, in that moment, Luke believed Little Luke had been born to replace him."

Evelyn reached over to pat Caitlin's hand. Caitlin's fidgeting had turned into full-blown restlessness, and she got up to make tea.

"He was quiet for the rest of the shopping trip and on the way home. I was unloading the car when he told me he didn't want to be called Junior anymore. I said, 'Okay, we'll call you Luke from now on.' I knew this had something to do with the incident in the grocery store, but I didn't know what.

"He said, 'I don't want to be Luke, either.' I could see his heart was broken. It was unkind of Nora Jean to choose that name for her son. And unconscionable for Big Luke to allow it. I didn't know what to do to make it right. So I said, 'Then we'll call you Lucky because I'm so lucky to have you.'

"If he can't see how Lucky he is to have you, Cait, then he doesn't deserve you. But you're going to have to find it in your heart to forgive him, because that's something he's never going to forgive of himself."

CHAPTER TWELVE

THE NEXT DAY CAITLIN called Bruce just to hear a friendly voice. "What's up?" he asked. "The big guy treating you all right?"

Big Guy. Little Guy.

"I can't make sense of any of this, Bruce." So she told him. Everything. CryoBank. Calhoun's sperm, his baby, everything.

"You don't sound surprised."

"Lucky didn't tell me. I guessed."

"Do you know what this would do to Nora Jean? It would devastate her. And I feel as if I somehow tainted my husband's memory. And why does it have to be that Calhoun hates the man I loved so much?"

She explained to Bruce what she had seen on the motocross tapes.

"I think I might have something to ease your mind on that score." It took him several minutes to find and send the file he was looking for. "I captured this on my cell phone a couple weeks before Luke died."

It was a basketball game. A night game from the look of it. Just a couple of three-on-three teams shooting hoops.

Luke was on one team. Calhoun on the other.

"Why am I watching this?"

Calhoun was aggressive. Used foul language. And went after Luke every chance he got. In short, he was a bully. And on one particular play where Luke had the ball, Calhoun stole it with a shoulder hit that knocked the ball away from Luke. Luke hit the ground hard.

A whistle blew and a foul was called. "Just keep watching," Bruce said.

Action stopped for a moment. Calhoun was breathing heavily from exertion. Sweating, he paced in a circle. When he turned to Luke, Calhoun reached down and helped Luke back to his feet.

Action resumed with Luke's free throws.

Caitlin heaved a sigh. "That makes me feel better," she said. Even if her heart ached just a little knowing that had probably been her husband's last basketball game.

THAT EVENING NORA JEAN CALLED to say she couldn't make it to that Thursday's Lamaze class. She had her monthly bereavement meeting in Colorado Springs with other mothers of fallen soldiers.

Caitlin left a note for Calhoun.

She was already sitting on her mat alone in class when she saw him, a silhouette in the door frame. She caught her breath.

He removed his leather jacket and joined her on the floor. Her heart knew a moment of pure joy. There was only one person who belonged in the delivery room with her.

"Hey, Coach," she said, trying to keep the mood light as he snuggled up against her backside.

"Hey," he responded, and she relaxed against him.

What would he say if she asked him to stay until after the baby was born? What would he say if she simply asked him to stay?

"YOU WANTED TO SEE ME?" Lucky asked as he stepped into Big Luke's office.

"We're getting good press on that new commercial." Big Luke put down the newspaper he'd been reading. "In fact, we're getting good press on the custom service we're offering. I think we should show off that bike of yours in the motor and boat show coming to town."

"Sounds good." His response sounded flat, even to his own ears. He stood there a moment with his hands tucked in the front pockets of his jeans. "Was there anything else?" he asked, already turning to leave.

"Yes," his father said, surprising him.

Lucky took a step back toward the desk. Instead of inviting him to sit, his father stood. Big Luke opened the glass-front cabinet that hid the wet bar. "Bought this the year you were born." He pulled out a bottle of Scotch and two glasses. "Think it's long past time we cracked it open."

Hearing something close to sentiment in the old man made Lucky shift uncomfortably. But he nodded.

Big Luke poured two tumblers and handed one to him. "I'm not going to be around forever. I'd like you to be part of the business." His father raised his glass expectantly.

Lucky had waited all his life to hear those words.

Sucking in air, he let it out again. "I can't," he said, feeling the weight of the tumbler in his hand.

"Calhoun and Sons. That's always been a dream of mine."

Big Luke looked up from swirling his drink. "I thought that was something we shared."

Lucky set his drink down on the desk. There'd be no celebrating today. "And I thought I'd made it clear that first day—I'm not here to stay." The words came out harsher than he'd intended.

The baby was due in less than a month.

And he'd be all out of excuses to stick around.

Even if Cait asked him to stay, she wasn't likely to acknowledge him as her baby's father. He might have access to her bed, but when she closed her eyes he had no illusions about who she was making love to.

Luke would always come between them.

Lucky had set out to do something right and he'd turned it into something very wrong. Everything he wanted was right here in his grasp. Cait, the baby, the business. If he could live with the fact that he didn't deserve it and the only reason he had it was that Luke was dead.

Big Luke cleared his throat. "Is this about that sign?" he asked, misinterpreting Lucky's silence. He put down his own glass. "Yes, I should have put up *Sons* so none of you boys felt slighted. But Bruce and Luke weren't the ones turning eighteen that year."

Lucky's throat burned—without the help of alcohol. "Why didn't you tell me?"

"When you were four, I divorced your mother. I didn't disown you or your brother. When you were eight, my brother started sleeping with my ex-wife. Yes, I was the one who'd had the affair with my secretary. She got pregnant. I got a divorce and married her, but only because your mother wouldn't have me back. I don't blame Evelyn for that. And I don't blame her for marrying a better man, even kin." He shook his head as if he were still in denial. "But if you think that wasn't a painful period for me, then you'd be wrong."

He perched on his desk. "I was wrong to put my pain above your welfare. But I kept up those support payments and you kids never went without. Business wasn't always this good—" he spread his arms to indicate everything around him "—and your mother didn't want any part of it. I paid her fair market value for the house so she could have her fresh start."

Lucky scrubbed a hand over the stubble on his head. His hand came to rest at the back of his neck. He couldn't tell if the tension was coming or going after his father's revelation.

"I was proud of you when you were a scrapper. And I'm proud of you now. I wasn't just blowing smoke when I said I'm not going to be around forever. I have lung cancer. I had it before. Now it's back. The doc doesn't think I'm going to be able to beat it this time, but what the hell does he know, right?"

It was as if he'd found and lost his father in the same instant. Thirty-two years of hurt and none of it mattered. His heart filled to capacity with forgiveness and yet ached with emptiness. "I don't know what to say."

"Say I'm leaving my business in good hands." His father clapped him on the shoulder. "You, Bruce, Luke's son. You're all I have left that matters."

Lucky closed his eyes and shook his head. "I can't," he said, his voice cracking. He glanced at the picture of Luke above his father's desk. "I can't stay here," he repeated.

His father's grip tightened and his voice boomed as he said, "I don't understand."

"Well, you'll understand this." Lucky shook off his father's grasp. "Cait's pregnant with *my* son."

Lucky waited for the accusations to fly.

Instead, his father looked at him with compassion.

Someone rapped on the glass. Both men turned in time to see Maddie standing there, frantic. And Nora Jean hurrying to the nearest exit.

"NORA." LUCKY CAUGHT UP with her and tried to explain, but she didn't want to listen. She got into her car and drove off.

And he knew where she was going. Lucky raced around back for his bike, then sped to the house.

Cait met him at the side porch. He looked up at her from the bottom step. "Nora Jean knows" was all he got out before Nora pulled her car into the driveway.

"Is it true?" she asked, coming after Cait.

Lucky put himself between them—Cait up on the porch and Nora Jean down on the gravel drive.

"Are you carrying Lucky's baby?" Luke's mother demanded.

"It's not like that, Nora," Lucky said, raising his voice above hers.

"It's nobody's fault," Cait added. "It's just something that happened. Their samples were switched. But this baby is as much Luke's as it is mine. Calhoun just supplied the DNA."

Ouch! Even if she'd just said it to appease her mother-in-law, it hurt. Made worse by the fact that he knew it was what she believed.

And Nora Jean seemed willing to accept it. The alternative for her would have been to have nothing of Luke left.

"So you never slept together," the woman said coolly.

Lucky and Cait locked gazes for a brief telltale second.

"I thought so," Nora Jean said, walking away.

Cait followed her, but nothing she could say would turn the woman back around. Then Cait turned on him. "Why? Why did you have to ruin everything?"

IT WAS UNFAIR OF HER TO BLAME him for something that wasn't his fault. It was unfair of her to throw him out.

But Cait didn't feel like being fair. She was too hurt.

She didn't love Calhoun. Not the way she'd loved Luke. And she'd keep telling herself that until she believed it.

A few days after he left, she tried to get her life back to normal. Of course, she couldn't remember what that had been. So she started with laundry.

From the laundry room, she had a view of the fenced-in backyard. A big backyard. With enough room for kids to run in and a swing set for them to play on. She could almost hear the screen door slamming behind the Calhoun boys as they ran outside to play.

There was a shelf above the washer/dryer stocked with laundry supplies and she tossed a couple of things into the washer.

Stryker followed on her heels. He whined a lot these days. And she couldn't blame him. She whined a lot, too.

She reached down to pet him. And when she stood back up she pressed a hand to the small of her back. That was getting harder to do.

Stryker sniffed around Calhoun's old seabag and whined again. The dog could probably still smell him. Then the dog lifted his leg and peed. Right on Calhoun's seabag.

"Bad dog, bad dog," Caitlin said, picking him up and taking him outside.

She came back in and cleaned the mess. And realized she'd have to empty the seabag and see what else in there was damaged.

She opened his padlock—he'd left the key in the lock—and dug through his clean laundry on top. She'd forgotten he'd washed all his uniforms right after he'd returned from Iraq.

She brought one of those clean T-shirts to her nose. Not a trace of his scent. At least not to her nose. Suddenly, she envied Stryker.

About halfway down she uncovered a book. *What To Expect When You're Expecting.* She had a copy, as well, but was surprised he had one. Tucked inside were two letters and a receipt.

She recognized the receipt as payment in full for her engagement ring. She clutched the ring and his dog tags around her neck and sank to the floor.

The first letter was addressed to her. Just her name scrawled across the envelope in his big bold handwriting.

Caitlin opened the letter, feeling like the intruder that she was. Even though it was addressed to her, he'd never given it to her. She read it out loud.

Dear Cait,

Today you told me I was going to be a father. I guess the word we're using is *donor.* I'm afraid I may have come across as a little abrupt during our conversation. There were just so many things going through my mind. Not the least of which was your welfare, and that of the baby.

Our convoy has been sidelined by a sandstorm. I can't

see two feet in front of my face, but here I sit scribbling out a note with my nubby pencil because I can't stop thinking about you and wondering if you're all right.

For me war is kind of like this storm. Something to be weathered. You take it as it comes and you never know how it's going to be until you're in it. Then all you can do is wait it out.

I guess that could be said of life in general.

I'm sorry you're having to go through all that alone. I want you to know that I'm here for you.

Sometimes we just have to wait and see how things turn out. When I think about the baby, I want more than anything to be a part of his or her life. But for now all I can do is wait.

Should anything happen to me, my brother, Bruce, will be contacting you regarding my last will and testament. I'm leaving everything to you and the baby.

You're probably wondering how it is that your husband had a half brother, two half brothers, that you knew nothing about. We grew up in separate families, not always on the best of terms.

If I have one regret it's that I never got to know Luke as a brother. The only thing that would eclipse that now is if I never got the chance to see the baby.

He'd signed it, "Always, Lucky."

Cait glanced at the receipt again and at the sealed letter addressed to Peanut. She hugged them to her breast as she imagined his convoy stopped along the road in a sandstorm. From day one, and under the most deplorable conditions, he'd put her first. Even when it conflicted with his own desires.

When was she going to admit she loved him?

And had for a long time.

"One last gift, Luke," Caitlin said, staring up at the ceiling. "I don't think I fully appreciated the one you sent me after my other request. So could you, please, turn him around and bring him home? I'm pretty sure he's halfway to Sturgis by now."

THAT THURSDAY EVENING, the nineteenth of June, Caitlin went to her Lamaze class alone. She didn't expect Nora Jean to be there. Her mother-in-law wasn't even returning her calls. But she kept glancing at the door, hoping Calhoun would show up.

Fifteen minutes into class, still watching the door, she felt her heart skip a beat when she glanced up and saw Evelyn standing there.

"I thought you might need a coach," the woman said, joining her on the mat.

"Thank you." Holding back tears of gratitude, Caitlin hugged Lucky's mother.

After class they stopped by Dairy Queen for Peanut Buster Parfaits. The first contraction followed the first bite. Caitlin forgot about eating ice cream and sank back in the chair.

"Are you all right?" Evelyn asked.

"Just Braxton Hicks, I think."

The next contraction came ten minutes later and Evelyn started timing them with the stopwatch she'd brought to class.

"Let's move around to see if they subside," she suggested. "If not, then we know it's the real thing."

Caitlin took her parfait with her and didn't have any more

contractions on the way to her car, but the pain in her lower back intensified.

"I'm going to follow you home," Evelyn said from the open driver-side door of her Explorer. Their parking spaces were side by side. Caitlin had the top down on the Mustang and was already behind the wheel.

"I'll be fine," she insisted. "This baby's not coming until Saturday."

"Saturday?" Evelyn closed her car door and walked over to the passenger side of Caitlin's car. She looked up at the sky. "There's a full moon. I wouldn't be surprised if this baby comes tonight."

"Isn't that just an old wives' tale?"

"They don't get to be old wives' tales without some truth to them. I've been around enough maternity wards to know."

"I'm still holding out for Saturday." Saturday was the first day of summer and the baby's due date.

"Only a small percentage of babies are born on their due date, Cait."

"It's the anniversary of Luke's death. And *Lucky* will be home that day," she said with confidence, even though she didn't know for certain.

Evelyn offered a sad smile. She didn't say she doubted it, but Caitlin knew that's what his mother was thinking. No one had been able to reach him on his cell phone, not even Bruce, since the day Cait kicked him out. "He'd better be" was all Evelyn said.

"When did he tell you about the baby?" Caitlin knew Evelyn's appearance tonight was no coincidence, but she'd thought the woman had probably heard from Dottie or Nora Jean.

"Oh, honey, a mother just knows these things." Evelyn opened the passenger door of the Mustang and slid in next to Cait to give her a hug.

"Do you think it's possible to love two brothers at the same time?" Caitlin asked.

"Well, now, you're asking an authority, aren't you?" Evelyn smiled. "Although I'd have to say I'd fallen out of love with Big Luke long before I fell in love with John. But Big Luke still tugs at my heartstrings, especially when I'm feeling nostalgic. And I think I was attracted to John the moment I met him in Vietnam."

"You met John in Vietnam?"

"Uh-huh," Evelyn confirmed. "China Beach. Luke, too. It was the early seventies. Dottie and I were Navy nurses serving the Marines. We were good friends and she introduced me to her brothers the night of a big Bob Hope USO show. John was late getting there because he'd been out on patrol and the crowd packed the airplane hangar so he had a hard time finding us. By then Luke and I had hit it off. But I remember feeling butterflies when we were introduced."

Cait took the lid off her parfait and started spooning it into her mouth as she listened.

"Years later when I was a divorced mother of two," Evelyn continued, "John helped me through the worst of it. Then one day, out of the blue, he said, 'I wish I'd gotten there first,' and I knew." Evelyn put a hand to her heart. "I knew I'd been in love with him for a long time, but I count that as the moment I fell in love with him."

"It can happen like that, can't it?" Caitlin said, speaking from experience. "You explain away the butterflies when you first meet him at the airport because it's wrong. Then the next thing you know it's…too late."

"It's never too late, Cait," Evelyn said, brushing the hair back from Cait's face. "Win or lose, it's only a tragedy if you let it become one by not taking a risk. Do you know why the boys call Dottie their crazy aunt?"

Cait shook her head.

"John brought a buddy with him the night of the USO show, a Corporal Eastbrook. For Dottie it was love at first sight. They got engaged, and a short while later he was killed. A year of grieving is expected, a couple years romantic. But romantic love is not real love, and thirty years wasted is sad."

I'm Dottie, Cait thought as she drove home.

Or at least she'd planned on being just like Dottie, but with a baby to ease the loneliness. What kind of burden was that to put on a child? And how selfish was she to choose a dead father or no father over her baby's real father?

Cait pulled into her driveway behind an SUV. The new Suzuki XL7 was a mobile advertisement for Calhoun Cycles and Suzuki motorcycles and parts. Just like the one Calhoun had said he'd get for her. Her heart raced as she hurried to get out of the car. There were no lights on in the house or the shed. Or even the garage he'd built.

There was an envelope tucked under the windshield wiper. She tore into it as Evelyn came up behind her. The note was from Big Luke. "This came for you today" was all it said.

Cait tipped the torn envelope, looking for a key.

She opened the unlocked car door. She looked under the floor mat and flipped down the visor. The keys fell into her hands. She was backing out the door when she noticed the baby seat in back.

"He really does think of everything," she murmured, closing the car door.

Please let him realize she needed him home.

Mounting the stairs to her house, Caitlin glanced at the shed. "What do you suppose FOB stands for?"

"Forward Operating Base," the other woman said.

"Hmm." It still didn't make any sense to her. But it must have made sense to him.

"You call me if those contractions start up again," Evelyn insisted. "Otherwise I'll call you tomorrow. Good night."

"Night." That night, instead of sleeping in the house, Caitlin and Stryker curled up on the cot in the FOB. Other than the neatly made bed and unplugged appliances, there was nothing belonging to Calhoun. He'd taken all his civilian clothes. His seabag full of uniforms he no longer needed was still in her laundry room. But his pillow smelled of him, so she held on to it.

FRIDAY MORNING Dottie and Evelyn showed up with overnight bags in hand to let Caitlin know they meant business. "Either we stay here until you go into labor," Evelyn said, "or you come home with one of us."

"You can't stay here alone," Dottie agreed.

Since that wasn't an option right now, Caitlin packed a suitcase. She added the Babies R Us bag with the Big Guy/Little Guy T-shirts.

Evelyn offered an indulgent smile. But both Evelyn and Dottie looked at her as if she was crazy when she pulled Luke's flag out of the triangular display box.

"I'd like to stop by Nora Jean's on the way to the hospital."

"Hospital?" Evelyn said, catching on quickly.

"Since about four this morning," Caitlin confirmed. Her contractions had been coming at regular two-minute intervals for at least three hours. But they hadn't intensified until she was up and moving.

"You should have called me," Evelyn scolded.

"First babies don't come that fast, right?" Evelyn and Dottie hurried her out to the car. "Stryker!" Cait said, turning back.

"Leave your house key. We'll have Keith come by and take the dog over to our place," Evelyn said, turning Cait back toward the Explorer. "Have you called your doctor?"

Caitlin called her doctor. And tried Lucky one last time. His phone went straight to voice mail, as it had for the past week. When she hung up she had to argue with Evelyn to get her headed in the direction of Nora Jean's house. "This is really important to me."

Caitlin got out of the car and waited for another contraction to subside. Evelyn and Dottie started to get out, too, but she waved them back and walked to the door. She rang the doorbell and waited.

Nora Jean answered. "What do you want?" she asked, tight-lipped.

"Here," Caitlin said, holding out Luke's flag, "I want you to have this. I know how much it means to you...." The woman accepted it as her due. "I just don't think you know how much it means to me."

"Oh, please," Nora Jean said.

"I'm sorry, I never meant to deceive you. I was trying to fill a lonely place." Caitlin took a deep breath and waited for another contraction to pass. "I will always love him, Nora.

This baby, Lucky's baby, should bring us—" she included Dottie and Evelyn, who were hurrying toward her "—closer together as a family, not tear us apart. You still have two stepsons, and you're about to have a step-grandbaby. You don't have to feel alone."

"Your step-*grandbaby*," Evelyn said, "is going to be born on your front stoop if you don't forgive this girl right now."

"Come on," Dottie said, ushering everyone toward the car, "Cait can explain genetics to you on the way to the hospital."

LUCKY HAD THROWN his cell phone out somewhere over the San Juan mountains. He'd spent the week exploring the scenic back roads of western Colorado from Black Canyon to Yampa Valley. He'd spent last night in Grand Junction at the Best Western.

After a hearty breakfast Lucky made up his mind to move on.

He'd promised himself a year of doing nothing and going nowhere, and that's what he intended to do. Eventually he'd find out from Bruce when the baby was born and maybe he'd stop by next year on the kid's first birthday.

He could do this. He could be Uncle Lucky.

Because that's the only option she'd left him.

But by the time he'd hit Utah he had a new plan.

He couldn't stop thinking ahead to next year. And going nowhere and doing nothing didn't sound like much of an existence. There was only one way to ensure he stayed away from Cait.

Lucky got off the highway at the next exit and pulled into the nearest gas station. The pay phone had been ripped off the wire, but he found what he was looking for in the Yellow Pages.

Twenty minutes later he pulled into a strip mall and up to a storefront Marine Corps recruiting station. He parked his bike and headed to the Cingular Wireless next door, where he bought a new cell phone and reactivated his service. Afterward he stopped by the recruiting station for a quick chat with the recruiter. He'd been out of the service less than ninety days. There'd be no problem reactivating his military service, either.

On the other side of the recruiting station he saw a pawnshop and a tattoo parlor. He skipped the pawnshop and sketched out a rough drawing for the tattoo artist. "Like you're looking through the crosshairs," he explained to the guy, who went by the name of Dice.

"I usually advise against names. Leaves an ugly scar when you try to have it removed." Dice snapped on latex gloves.

"Do I look like I care?" Lucky asked, taking off his shirt.

Dice smiled, showing off a gold tooth. "Where you want it?"

Lucky pointed to the left of his heart.

"So what did this Cait do to you?"

"Nothing."

Lucky was putting his shirt back on when he caught a glimpse of the newspaper. "That today's?"

"Yeah," Dice confirmed, ringing up the sale.

Lucky paid the three hundred dollars for the tat and left. At least he hadn't made it all the way to the coast before realizing what an idiot he was.

Tomorrow was the anniversary of Luke's death. He'd just call to make sure Cait was all right. When he couldn't get in touch with her at home or on her cell, he started to worry.

He'd tossed out his entire phone book with his old cell

phone. So he called the few numbers he had memorized and left messages. While waiting for return calls, he stepped inside the pawnshop and looked for something that might be appropriate for a mother-to-be.

"Can I see that?" He pointed to a blue sapphire necklace.

The gal behind the counter pulled out the tray. The necklace was nothing special and he skipped over it to admire a diamond-studded, horseshoe-shaped ring. It was a man's ring and not what he was looking for. Curious about the assortment of wedding bands that wound up in a pawnshop, he looked them over.

There was a platinum band in Cait's size. Lucky read the Latin inscription—*Semper Fi*.

Always Faithful was the Marine Corps motto.

His cell phone rang and he put the wedding band aside. "Hello?"

"Where the hell are you?" Big Luke demanded.

"Utah."

"Get your ass home. Cait went into labor this morning."

Lucky's heart beat against his chest. Or maybe that was just the throb of his new tattoo. "She okay?" he asked, stepping outside.

"She's fine."

"She ask for me?"

"What do you think?"

"I think if she doesn't want me there I shouldn't be there," he said, stopping himself from bolting for his bike.

"What do you want?" his father asked.

His old man couldn't see him shaking his head. "It doesn't matter what I want."

"No, it sure the hell doesn't. So get over yourself. And do right by your son. Just because it hurts that Cait doesn't want you there doesn't mean you shouldn't be there." His father's voice softened as he added, "Sometimes the hard thing is the right thing."

LUCKY WAS PULLED OVER by the Utah Highway Patrol on I-15 North. If the guy hadn't been on a motorcycle, well, Lucky would have seriously considered outrunning him.

"Driver's license and registration, please."

"Look, my *wife* is in labor," he lied for the sake of expediency.

"Like I haven't heard that one before."

"I'm just trying to catch the first flight out of Salt Lake to Denver so I can be there."

"Do you know why I pulled you over, sir?"

Speeding. "You're not ex-military…. Never been to Iraq… You're not going to give me a break, are you?"

"No."

"Didn't think so." He handed over his license.

"Eighty in a fifty-five. Weaving in and out of traffic. Speeding. Careless driving… Your wife's going to thank me for pulling you over."

"That would be my ex-wife. Thanks," Lucky said, accepting the ticket.

The officer tipped his hat, got back on his bike and tailed Lucky all the way to Salt Lake City International Airport. Lucky didn't dare exceed the posted speed limit of fifty-five.

"Sir, you can't park there." The officer pulled in right behind him.

"Watch me."

"Sir, I'm going to have your vehicle towed."

"I figured that from the sign." No Parking, Tow Away Zone. "Look, the key is in the ignition. The title is under the seat." He stepped back, got it out and signed it. "It's yours. Do whatever the hell you want with it," Lucky said, walking away from his first custom bike. After this he was probably going to lose his license, anyway.

"CAIT?" CALHOUN KNOCKED on the partially open door.

She tensed with the next contraction, then relaxed against the pillow. "What took you so long?"

"Ladies, can you excuse us?" he asked the other women in the room. Dottie put away her knitting and Nora Jean abandoned her book. His mother was the last to leave them alone.

He closed the door and stood there with his hands in his pockets, looking around. It was supposed to look like a bedroom, but it looked like what it was—a labor and delivery room.

She dropped her feet over the side of the bed.

"Don't get up," he said, rushing to her side.

"I'm supposed to move around." But she didn't get up.

He pulled up a chair and sat down. Bowing his head over her belly, he held her at the waist. "I can't be this baby's uncle, Cait, because I need to be his father. Whether you want me or not, Cait, I'm Peanut's dad."

"Look at me," she said, brushing her fingers through his hair. "I want you to see the exact moment I fell in love with you."

He raised his head to look at her. If he hadn't been a hardened Marine all those years, she'd say the wonder in his eyes looked suspiciously like tears.

"Lucky…I love you," she said.

He pushed to his feet and leaned in to kiss her.

She pulled back. "You're supposed to say you love me, too."

He continued to lean in until his lips were pressed against hers. "I love you, too, Cait."

He pulled back with the next contraction.

"I'm not a screamer," she said, "but I'm twenty hours into this labor and don't think the epidural is working. Ahhh…!" She clutched at his leather jacket and they breathed through the contraction together.

When she let go, he reached into his breast pocket and pulled out a platinum wedding band. He slipped it on her finger next to her engagement ring. "You know you're supposed to ask me first," she gasped.

"Marry me, Cait."

She looked down at her hand. "I'll always love him. And sometimes I don't know where my life with him ended and where my life with you began, but—" she looked into his eyes "—I promise you this, I will *always* love you, too."

"Is that a yes?" he asked.

She wiped away tears. "I'm not a crier."

"I have news for you, Cait. You're a crier."

"And a screamer." She clutched his shoulder. "I think it's time to get the doctor in here…nowwwwwww!"

IT'S A LITTLE DRIBBLER!
CHANCE LANE CALHOUN
June 21, 2008 0102 Hours
height: 22 inches

weight: 7 pounds 7 ounces
FATHER LUKE CHANCE CALHOUN JUNIOR
MOTHER CAITLIN EILEEN EVERETT CALHOUN

EPILOGUE

Eighteen months later…

BETWEEN THE RESERVE DRILLS—yes, he'd reenlisted—and the business trips, he was gone more often than Caitlin would have liked. But that only made the homecomings sweeter.

"Which one is daddy?" Caitlin asked.

Her son pointed his chubby baby finger right at Lucky. "Daddy," Chance whined, contorting his chubby little body.

Lucky, his seabag slung over his shoulder, headed straight for them with a red rose in his hand. "Hey, little guy," he said, taking the baby from her.

"Hey, big guy." They exchanged a kiss for her rose.

As good as he looked in that uniform or in his business suit, she liked him best in his coveralls with grease under his nails. Because that's when he was home, with her and the baby, working on his bikes.

"I have something for you." He patted his pocket.

"I have something for you, too," she said suggestively.

"Don't you want to know what it is?" He reached into his pocket and pulled out a sizable check.

"Another tattoo with my name? Or a ring from a pawnshop?" she teased. She loved the pawnshop ring. And his reason for buying it.

Every ring had a story to tell, including her engagement ring. She hated the tattoo—a shot through the heart with her name on it. She didn't like being reminded that she'd hurt him. But she did like being reminded that he loved her in a very permanent way.

In any case, she'd live with it because she loved him.

"The Utah Highway patrol contracted for twelve of my custom bikes."

"Still thinking of expanding the company?" With Big Luke going into semiretirement after his third divorce and his second remission from cancer, Lucky had taken over the family business.

Chance rested his sleepy head against his daddy's broad shoulder. Lucky looked down at his son, then her.

"More like expanding the family. Calhoun and *Sons* has a nice ring to it."

"And what about *daughters?*"

He waggled his eyebrows. "Tell me again how lucky I am."

* * * * *

Enjoy a sneak preview of
MATCHMAKING WITH A MISSION
by B.J. Daniels,
part of the WHITEHORSE, MONTANA *miniseries.*
Available from Harlequin Intrigue
in April 2008.

Nate Dempsey has returned to Whitehorse to uncover the truth about his past...

Nate sensed someone watching the house and looked out in surprise to see a woman astride a paint horse just on the other side of the fence. He quickly stepped back from the filthy second-floor window, although he doubted she could have seen him. Only a little of the June sun pierced the dirty glass to glow on the dust-coated floor at his feet as he waited a few heartbeats before he looked out again.

The place was so isolated he hadn't expected to see another soul. Like the front yard, the dirt road was waist-high with weeds. When he'd broken the lock on the back door, he'd had to kick aside a pile of rotten leaves that had blown in from last fall.

As he sneaked a look, he saw that she was still there, staring at the house in a way that unnerved him. He shielded his eyes from the glare of the sun off the dirty window and studied her, taking in her head of long blond hair that feathered out in the breeze from under her Western straw hat.

She wore a tan canvas jacket, jeans and boots. But it was

the way she sat astride the brown-and-white horse that nudged the memory.

He felt a chill as he realized he'd seen her before. In that very spot. She'd been just a kid then. A kid on a pretty paint horse. Not this one—the markings were different. Anyway, it couldn't have been the same horse, considering the last time he had seen her was more than twenty years ago. That horse would be dead by now.

His mind argued it probably wasn't even the same girl. But he knew better. It was the way she sat on the horse, so at home in a saddle and secure in her world on the other side of that fence.

To the boy he'd been, she and her horse had represented freedom, a freedom he'd known he would never have—even after he escaped this house.

Nate saw her shift in the saddle, and for a moment he feared she planned to dismount and come toward the house. With Ellis Harper in his grave, there would be little to keep her away.

To his relief, she reined her horse around and rode back the way she'd come.

As he watched her ride away, he thought about the way she'd stared at the house—today and years ago. While the smartest thing she could do was to stay clear of this house, he had a feeling she'd be back.

Finding out her name should prove easy, since he figured she must live close by. As for her interest in Harper House… He would just have to make sure it didn't become a problem.

* * * * *

Be sure to look for
MATCHMAKING WITH A MISSION
and other suspenseful Harlequin Intrigue stories,
available in April
wherever books are sold.

HARLEQUIN® Romance®

presents

The Wedding Planners

Planning perfect weddings... finding happy endings!

Amidst the rustle of satins and silks, the scent of red roses and white lilies and the excited chatter of brides-to-be, six friends from Boston are The Wedding Belles—they make other people's wedding dreams come true....

But are they always the wedding planner...never the bride?

Who will be the next to say "I do"?

In April: Shirley Jump, *Sweetheart Lost and Found*
In May: Myrna Mackenzie, *The Heir's Convenient Wife*
In June: Melissa McClone, *S.O.S. Marry Me*
In July: Linda Goodnight, *Winning the Single Mom's Heart*
In August: Susan Meier, *Millionaire Dad, Nanny Needed!*
In September: Melissa James, *The Bridegroom's Secret*

And don't miss the exciting wedding-planner tips and author reminiscences that accompany each book!

www.eHarlequin.com HR17507

Silhouette

SPECIAL EDITION™

Introducing a brand-new miniseries

Men of
Mercy Medical

Gabe Thorne moved to Las Vegas to open a
new branch of his booming construction
business—and escape from a recent tragedy.
But when his teenage sister showed up pregnant
on his doorstep, he really had his hands full.
Luckily, in turning to Dr. Rebecca Hamilton for
the medical care his sister needed, he found
a cure for himself....

Starting with

THE MILLIONAIRE
AND THE M.D.

by *TERESA SOUTHWICK,*

available in April wherever books are sold.

REQUEST YOUR FREE BOOKS!

2 FREE NOVELS PLUS 2 FREE GIFTS!

HARLEQUIN®

Super Romance®

Exciting, emotional, unexpected!

YES! Please send me 2 FREE Harlequin Superromance® novels and my 2 FREE gifts (gifts are worth about $10). After receiving them, if I don't wish to receive any more books, I can return the shipping statement marked "cancel." If I don't cancel, I will receive 6 brand-new novels every month and be billed just $4.69 per book in the U.S. or $5.24 per book in Canada, plus 25¢ shipping and handling per book and applicable taxes, if any*. That's a savings of close to 15% off the cover price! I understand that accepting the 2 free books and gifts places me under no obligation to buy anything. I can always return a shipment and cancel at any time. Even if I never buy another book from Harlequin, the two free books and gifts are mine to keep forever.

135 HDN EEX7   336 HDN EEYK

Name	(PLEASE PRINT)	
Address		Apt. #
City	State/Prov.	Zip/Postal Code

Signature (if under 18, a parent or guardian must sign)

Mail to the Harlequin Reader Service:
IN U.S.A.: P.O. Box 1867, Buffalo, NY 14240-1867
IN CANADA: P.O. Box 609, Fort Erie, Ontario L2A 5X3

Not valid to current subscribers of Harlequin Superromance books.

Want to try two free books from another line?
Call 1-800-873-8635 or visit www.morefreebooks.com.

* Terms and prices subject to change without notice. N.Y. residents add applicable sales tax. Canadian residents will be charged applicable provincial taxes and GST. This offer is limited to one order per household. All orders subject to approval. Credit or debit balances in a customer's account(s) may be offset by any other outstanding balance owed by or to the customer. Please allow 4 to 6 weeks for delivery. Offer available while quantities last.

Your Privacy: Harlequin is committed to protecting your privacy. Our Privacy Policy is available online at www.eHarlequin.com or upon request from the Reader Service. From time to time we make our lists of customers available to reputable third parties who may have a product or service of interest to you. If you would prefer we not share your name and address, please check here. ☐

HSR08

HARLEQUIN *Presents*

He's successful, powerful—and extremely sexy....
He also happens to be her boss! Used to getting his
own way, he'll demand what he wants from her—
in the boardroom and the bedroom....

Watch the sparks fly as these couples
work together—and play together!

IN BED WITH
THE BOSS

Don't miss any of the stories in April's collection!

MISTRESS IN PRIVATE
by JULIE COHEN

IN BED WITH HER ITALIAN BOSS
by KATE HARDY

MY TALL DARK GREEK BOSS
by ANNA CLEARY

HOUSEKEEPER TO
THE MILLIONAIRE
by LUCY MONROE

Available April 8
wherever books are sold.

HPP0408NEW

HARLEQUIN *Super Romance*

COMING NEXT MONTH